Of Ashes and Chaos

A Poppy Seymour Mystery

K. S. Roberson

Contents

I

Magical
Medical
Miracles

THE ENVELOPE WAS A bright, violent red, juxtaposed with royal gold embossed sides. The whole letter glimmered in the pile of otherwise bland and boring bills. The handwriting across the front was spindly, the words strung together like cobwebs floating in the air.

I stared down at my name, frozen in time on the letter: *Poppy Seymour, 3848 Elmswood Drive.* The return address was blank.

"Are you ever going to open it?" Agnes asked, from beside me. "I'm not getting any deader." She gave a dramatic huff that caused some of her whispy, gray hair to fluff out around her, escaping from the elegant French twist she normally kept in pristine order on top of her head. She was thin, with an angular face that somehow didn't show a single wrinkle, though currently, it was screwed up in distaste, her thin lips pursed. Oh, and she had been dead for fifty years. She had passed away at the ripe old age of 95, probably harping at someone. So, it wasn't like her death was a recent or tragic occurrence.

Some witches have good familiars. Cute cats with white and brown speckled fur. Others have toads, that while slimy have the advantage of catching flies and mosquitos, so you don't ever have to worry about bug spray. Not me. I've got Agnes. My great, great aunt.

Agnes had the personality of a cuttlefish, mixed with the attention span of a gnat. She was unfriendly and antisocial on a good day, and downright hostile and combative on the bad days.

Having her as my familiar was about as fun as cleaning your ear out with a cattle prod.

Everyone says that you earn your familiar. I don't know what I did to piss off the witches of old, but Agnes must have been the ultimate sin.

I blew out an unsteady breath, running a hand through my flyaway curly auburn hair, my skin sweating. I felt like a child, not a grown woman in her late twenties.

The letter trembled in my nervous fingers. I had been waiting for this.

And yet...

The cold feeling of trepidation was like ice flowing through my veins, causing goosebumps to erupt along my arms. What if it wasn't the answer I was hoping for?

"Oh my god! Open it already, you unhinged dunderhead. You're so sweaty, the ink is running. It's not like it's going to bite!"

Good old Agnes.

I ripped the seam of the letter open and stared down at the scalloped-edged, cream and gold invitation.

Dearest Miss Seymour, it read in the same delicate writing as the front.

I was delighted to read your letter, and I believe I can offer you a solution to your current predicament. As you may know, I am renown for my prowess in solving the unsolvable. In taking cases, like yours, and working miracles. In transforming lives. In being the best hope. Please accept my invitation to my humble abode to discuss your case with some other like-minded and equally needy individuals. In four days I can dramatically change your life. Please allow me the honor of doing so.

Sincerely,

Garret Goul,

Magical Medical Practice.

"Yes," I breathed softly, the air escaping my lungs in a soft hiss.

"Yes, what?" Agnes barked in my ear, making my eardrums ring. Agnes had a pitch to her voice that resonated like a gong. It reverberated in my head and made my eyes cross like a character in an old cartoon.

"I got in!" I sang, gleefully.

"Good grief. Would you please put a lid on that excitement and squash it back in?" Agnes griped, turning away. "It's like watching a kitten play with a ball of yarn."

"Agnes," I said, my voice still high-pitched with excitement. "Don't you realize what this means?"

"Of course. You'll finally be a bona fide witch, rather than the laughingstock of the coven. Blah, blah, blah."

OK, ouch. But here's the deal. Agnes wasn't wrong.

You see, I was born a witch. Into a very witchy family, whose main job was, you guessed it, to do witchy things.

We read tarot cards to see the future. We mix love potions, sleeping potions, and healing potions. We cast spells on innocent bystanders—nothing too nefarious, just casual movement or memory spells.

In the town of Rosehall, Washington, we were the ones who people went to when they needed a magical solution. Something outside the box. That was where we came in, where we shined.

Except for me. I was positive I was the worst witch in my coven.

Because I had the unfortunate and unmanageable problem of being born with Chaos.

What is Chaos?

It is exactly as it sounds. It means that every spell, every potion, every tarot card drawn was a lesson in futility.

When I'm supposed to read tarots, my readings are wildly off. Perhaps a card tells me that a person is going to find true love if they leave doors open. It could just as easily mean that a rabid cougar will wander into their house through that unlocked door.

When I was supposed to make a love potion—one to make the woman's significant other passionate and full of lust—I made one that made her grow a mustache. Unintentionally, of course.

When I was supposed to cast a spell to help cure a drought, I instead ended up summoning a swarm of cicadas that plagued the town for days. Never mind that Western Washington doesn't have cicadas.

Does everyone in the area still talk about the swarming bugs?

Yes.

Did it end up on the news, where local biologists discussed the ramifications of invasive species infestations?

Of course.

Does anyone come to me for any type of spell, reading, or potion anymore?

No. Not that I blame them.

And the rest of my coven? Well, they aren't too enamored with my magic either.

Chaos magic is uncommon and uncomfortable. Once in a generation, this type of magic will rear its ugly head. I was just the poor unfortunate soul that it happened to.

But that was all about to change.

Thanks to Garret Goul.

The Magical Medical Doctor.

The one who specialized in fixing the unfixable. The abnormal of their covens or packs, or whatever vampire groups were called.

Goul had arrived in Rosehall six months ago and advertised his services on the ivy-covered, brick walls of the library. He had zero takers.

But slowly, the magical misfits began to be cured of their ailments. And that trickle had turned into a stream. And they had all credited Garret Goul for the change.

Now, his business was so successful that he didn't even have to advertise. Instead, he sent out personalized invitations to his mansion. Offering to help those who had magical afflictions. And I had just secured the proverbial golden ticket. The invitations were highly coveted. Everyone who had received one and had gone through treatment said that their life was changed. And now, it was my turn.

My phone buzzed like an angry hornet, startling me enough to drop my invitation in the silence. I let out a shaky breath and then answered. "H-hello?"

"Did you pick up my dry cleaning?" My mother's voice barked across the line, her tone sharper than a steak knife cutting through butter.

"Mom?"

"Oh, Poppy, please tell me you didn't turn the dry cleaner into a mouse again. You know it's hard for him to get my suits done correctly if he's a mouse. I don't want more chew holes in my pockets. I need that charcoal gray pantsuit so I can wear it to the campaign dinner tonight."

And there it was, the titular reason why I wanted an invite to Garret Goul's house.

My mother.

My mother was the leader of our coven, the mayor of Rosehall (elected four times in a row), a great leader, the uniter of all magical races. She was a legend. She was perfection.

The only thing not perfect about her?

Me.

If I wanted to count the number of times my mother had had to fix my mistakes I would need to borrow the fingers and toes of everyone in town. "I didn't forget the dry cleaning," I said. "And Mr. Maple is fine. He's not a mouse or a raccoon or a skunk. I just..."

"Well then, what's the hold-up? I've been waiting for nearly an hour. Need I remind you how important this event is for me? It is an integral part of my campaign run. I need that suit for it."

"Well, I..."

"Never mind, can you get it here in five?" Her voice had risen ominously.

"Mom!" I snapped, my temper getting the better of me. But my mother pushed my buttons better than a rocketship on liftoff. "You're going to need to send someone else to go and get it. I can't do it."

There was a heavy silence on the other end of the line. I even checked the screen because I was certain she had hung up on me.

"You'd better have a good explanation, young lady." My mother's voice had gone steely. "When I gave you the job as my secretary, I thought it would be helpful for your situation. I hoped it would keep you out of trouble. But that tone is completely unwarranted. You are not seventeen. So act like it!"

"I got an invite from Garret Goul," I muttered into the void "I leave tomorrow."

More silence. I swear my mother wasn't even breathing on the other end of the phone.

I liked to believe that at her core, Serenity Seymour loved me. She may not have been one to show it outright, with grand gestures and meaningful conversations. Usually, her responses bordered on harsh and unfeeling. My mother was the perfect five-ten, blonde-haired, blue-eyed, model-thin politician, while I was shorter, at barely over five-three, with auburn hair that couldn't help but curl in all weather, and plain brown eyes. She was important in town, I was a nobody. She loved this town more than she loved her daughter.

I just wanted a mother to do my nails with. I wanted to believe that she thought of me with love and affection. Even if I was afflicted with the dreaded Chaos magic.

An invitation to Garret Goul's manor could spell success for her as well as for me. It could make it so she was no longer embarrassed by me. She could finally not be concerned that people would lose their fingers and toes around me, or be teleported to a bat cave in the middle of winter.

A win-win for both of us.

"Well," my mother cleared her throat. "That's good, I guess. I'm... I'm thrilled that he finally reached out! I've only heard good things."

"It'll take a few days for me to complete whatever course he has for me." I swallowed around the lump in my throat. "So I won't be in to work for at least four days, maybe a week."

"Yes, of course." My mother's tone had transitioned to bored and unaffected. As if she had already stopped paying attention.

"I'll call when I'm out of the program." And no longer an embarrassment to you.

"Of course." And with that, the line went dead. No "goodbye," no "I love you," just dead air.

"She's a right old witch," Agnes said from beside me, having listened in on my conversation. "Her mother would be ashamed of how she acts toward you."

It was the one thing that Agnes and I rarely agreed upon. She didn't like my mother, mostly because my mother had once called Agnes a "waste of a familiar," and then had asked why I couldn't do any better than that. When I responded that Agnes was good for me, Serenity had muttered under her breath, "a toadstool would have been better." Which, of course, cemented her status as persona non grata in Agnes's mind.

"Don't let her wackadoodle ways get to you," Agnes hissed. "We will have peace and quiet without her constant nagging. That woman should take a vow of silence! It would make everyone's life easier."

2

Garret Goul's Rules

Mischief Manor.

That was the name of Garret Goul's "house." Except it was a house in the same way that Buckingham Palace was considered a country home.

Mischief Manor had been constructed in the early 1900s by a witch who had deigned to marry a human. When her husband died suddenly of the Spanish Flu, leaving the woman a widow, she decided to go to a psychic, in the hopes of reconnecting with her dead husband. Instead, she learned that due to her husband's work weaponizing Mustard Gas in World War One, she was to be haunted by the spirits of those he had killed until the day she died. How it became her problem, I don't know. It seemed a little arbitrary.

The only way to combat this haunting was to continue to build onto her already massive home. Adding a bedroom here, a library there, a random door to midair: all of this was supposed to keep the vengeful spirits at bay and the remaining members of her family alive.

And so, she built Mischief Manor. A veritable labyrinth of a house, with 216 bedrooms, 45 bathrooms, and 1,457 doors. Mischief Manor looked like a birthday cake on a *Nailed It* special.

It was lopsided for one.

The whole house tilted to the left. Five large turrets stuck up at random points around the outside of the house. The siding was wood and had been painted white, though the paint was peeling and chipping off in places. The overall style of the house was Gothic, with arched windows, a huge wraparound porch, and a stark, burnt-umber roof.

The front of the house was immaculate. The grass was green and supple, and the hedges were trimmed neatly into little boxes. There wasn't a single leaf out of place. There was a wide curving driveway at the front of the house, like something out of a movie.

Large statues of Greek gods and goddesses hewn from white marble lined the driveway, their eyes all watching for new arrivals.

"Why are they staring at us?" Agnes asked in a hushed tone.

"They're not staring at us. They're statues." Even so, I was pretty sure that their blank eyes were following me as I walked up the driveway.

"I'm pretty sure the one in the toga just blinked."

"Please do not be alarmed," a deep voice echoed from behind me.

I nearly leaped out of my skin, whirling around.

A tall man, dressed in a crisp black suit with a white shirt, stood directly behind me. His jet-black hair was graying around the temples, he had piercing blue eyes set into ghostly pale skin, and his eyebrows dominated his face, like twin Wooly Bear caterpillars. His head tilted to the side as he observed me, which only served to freak me out more. I didn't do well with jumpscares, even when the person told me not to be alarmed.

"Are you Mr. Goul?" I asked once I'd found my voice.

Here's the thing. Garret Goul didn't go into town. It seemed as though he'd bought the house and disappeared inside it. He didn't go to any town functions. He didn't buy groceries or go out to eat. He didn't even go for a walk. He was a recluse. He simply existed inside his house, much like a daylight-scared vampire.

Only those who had gone through the program had ever seen him, and they didn't describe him in much detail. He was an enigma. A shadow floating through a giant mansion and curing the townfolk of their various ailments.

The man before me chuckled. His baritone voice conjured up thoughts of cigars and brandy. "No, Miss Seymour. I am Darcy, Mr. Goul's valet and right-hand man." He offered a thick hand for me to shake. "We are delighted to have you here. We are fascinated by the puzzle your affliction presents. I'm sure this experience will be very enlightening for you and your esteemed mother."

I certainly wasn't going to be telling my mother anything, even if she did deign to ask. I forced a smile, trying not to grimace at the mention of my mother. "Of course, I'm glad to get an invitation."

Darcy nodded sagely. "Now, there are a few rules—for lack of a better term—that you must abide by before entering the manor."

I cringed internally.

It wasn't like I was planning on writing a tell-all novel on what happened in the manor. I just didn't love the idea of having rules that governed my stay at a place that was supposed to be helpful. It made it feel like I was in rehab.

Darcy must have sensed my hesitation because he smiled gently. "It's not much, but we would like for you to forfeit your phone and any other electronic devices. Mr. Goul finds that in order for his program to be a success for our guests, they need to refrain from reaching out to their families and friends on a daily basis. Rest assured, if something occurs and a call is urgent, we will relay that to you. Second, no leaving the manor house while the program is in session. It is only for four days and we seal the doors, only opening them in case of emergency. Mr. Goul is the only one who knows the code. This is for your safety. And finally," Darcy continued, oblivious to my hesitation, "we ask that all guests stick to the common areas as much as possible. It is a large house, and I'm sure you know its history. There are many rooms that are booby-trapped or doors that open into thin air. We wouldn't want our guests injured during their stay here. Do you think you can abide by those rules?"

I wanted to say no. It sounded like house arrest in a house that could kill you for walking through the wrong door.

But then I pictured my mother's face. I could see her disappointment etched into the lines around her mouth every time she had to fix one of my mistakes. I didn't want to be Poppy-who-always-messes-up anymore.

I nodded, hesitantly. "I can do this."

Darcy flashed a wide smile that was all teeth. "Perfect! Welcome to Mischief Manor, Miss Seymour."

3

Wainscoting and Werewolves

AFTER HANDING OVER MY phone and signing an NDA that rivaled the Declaration of Independence, I was finally taken to my room. The sun was just beginning to kiss the horizon, the tell-tale signs of winter evident in the early setting of the sun.

Darcy navigated the house well. He didn't lead me through a single wrong door. He walked down the main hallways and pointed out various rooms as we passed. "This is the library. You are welcome to use it as we have a large assortment of texts and novels for guests to read. Mr. Goul especially likes scientific writing and the occasional thriller. And here is the observatory. If it's raining but you still want sunlight, you are welcome to take your morning coffee in there."

The house was centered around a large courtyard that had an extravagant fountain that depicted Lady Justice, half-dressed, holding her balance. The water burbled out of her mouth down into a pool that flowed into a pond at her feet. I could see flashes of color that had to be Koi swimming lazily by. Lily pads were visible floating primly on top of the water. The courtyard provided a space for fresh air to come into an otherwise locked up tight house. It made it easier to breathe.

Still, I didn't love the idea of being locked inside a mansion with only one way out. The whole thing screamed horror film, and I had seen enough of them to know that they typically didn't end well for the single girl. It wasn't even like I had a pet to save me, just Agnes.

And speaking of Agnes, she chose that moment to run into a framed picture on the wall, nearly knocking it off its hook. The picture shuddered violently, and I moved swiftly to catch it, pinning it back against the wall.

"What was that?" Darcy snapped, whirling toward the picture that was still swinging wildly, despite my best efforts.

I cringed. "Nothing."

Here was the deal.

Normally, I would tell people about Agnes. People seemed to feel more comfortable with me talking to myself when they realized I was actually talking to someone. Even if that someone was a ghost. So I typically tell people about her so that people don't think I'm carrying on a conversation with thin air. Also, when I called her a "flaming bag of old dog poop," they don't take offense.

I should have felt comfortable and at ease in the place where I was supposed to be getting help. But I didn't. Something about the house had my hair standing on end. Agnes was the only secret that I had that could be an ace-in-the-hole, if I needed one. "I'm a little clumsy," I lied.

Darcy's eyes narrowed, as though he could detect the fib. Then he asked casually, "Where is your familiar? I had anticipated needing a litter box or something to make your familiar's stay comfortable as well."

"Oh, mine died years ago," I said nonchalantly. "I haven't gotten around to replacing her yet." It wasn't a lie. Agnes had died decades ago. I couldn't replace her. I was stuck with her.

"I am sorry to hear that." Darcy turned and continued to my room, seeming to take me at my word. He stopped outside a dark wood door. "Dinner will be served in an hour in the Great Hall, which you can enter through the double doors opposite the library. Please be on time. Mr. Goul doesn't appreciate tardiness."

Well, he sounded like a load of fun.

"Thank you," I said, as I entered the stuffy room.

The first thing I noticed was the four-poster mahogany bed that dominated the room. The bed's hand-carved frame was adorned with tiny cherubs, their chubby little cheeks blowing kisses or looking surprised. Each cherub had a lock of hair that curled around their forehead and their hands were holding arrows.

"This is creepy," Agnes said from beside me. "Why does everything have a face?"

I silently agreed.

Across the room was a large wooden armoire with an old, cracked and dusty mirror. It had the same cherubs carved into its feet, making it look like they were straining to hold up the weight of the dresser.

"Haunted," Agnes said. "This room is 100% haunted."

"You're a ghost," I muttered.

"Then I would know! This place is freaky. And you want to stay here? What if there are vengeful spirits here? I can't fight off vengeful spirits. If they come for you, I'm leaving. I won't help you." She cast a dirty look at the cherubs.

"Would you have helped if the hypothetical spirits weren't vengeful?"

"Probably not, no."

"Good to know."

I hadn't packed too much. A couple of pairs of yoga pants, some tee shirts, and one black dress that I had thrown in at the last minute. I hadn't thought that I would need anything too formal, but I wanted to be prepared just in case I needed to look a little nicer. Yoga pants, while comfy, weren't the most formal attire.

I changed quickly and looked at myself in the mirror, straightening the hem of my dress. It probably would have been better if I had ironed it. But that was a lot of work considering I didn't own an iron.

"That's not going to make it any less wrinkled," Agnes said, examining me with a critical eye. "A steam bath would be better."

"Other than the wrinkles, does it look ok?"

"You're passable. Your mother wouldn't like it, but her sense of style is a bit like the three blind mice dressed Cinderella."

Oddly, that was a pretty apt way of describing it.

I squared my shoulders. "Showtime."

"It's not like you're going off to war."

***

The dining hall, because it was a hall, was massive. It had a long mahogany table that stretched from one wall to the other and could easily seat 30 people. Huge glittering chandeliers hung from the ceiling, their sides dripping with garish crystals. The walls were golden and had silver wainscoting. Large, gold-framed pictures sat at strategic intervals along the walls, depicting various garden scenes and more cherubs. The table was loaded with gold place settings, candelabras, and goblets. At the head of the table was a high-backed, gold velvet chair, and directly behind the chair was a large, taxidermy head of a lion.

There was only one other guest already seated at the table.

Dressed in an expensive-looking suit, the man had his head down, writing something on a little notepad. At the sound of my footsteps, he looked up.

Dark brown hair was cropped close to his head. His skin was a beautiful tawny, golden color, like he'd spent time outdoors. His jaw was sharp and his nose had a slight hook to it. He was large, tall, and broad-shouldered and his eyes were a beautiful green color with flecks of gold in the middle.

What made me draw up short wasn't his astonishing good looks. Not at all. Okay, that was a lie. His looks could stop traffic. In fact, I had seen his smile stop traffic.

Because I knew him. "Detective Banks," I said, quietly.

Silas Banks drew himself up to his full height, which was easily over six-two. A slight hint of a smile lit up his handsome face. "Ms. Seymour."

Silas Banks was considered the most eligible bachelor in the town. Not only was he a detective on our police force with a solid income and a stable job, he also had a face and a body that made even Agnes comment.

Since the police station was also located at City Hall, alongside my mother's office, I saw Silas often. Too often for my taste. The problem with Silas Banks wasn't anything to do with him, it was how ridiculously tongue-tied I got around him.

For example, one time he asked me how I was doing, and I answered, "I like sunchairs."

Yeah.

Sunchairs.

In response to the most basic "how are you?" on the planet.

So was it a surprise that when I saw him this time, my brain blanked again? I ended up blurting out, "But what is wrong with you?" I was about as smooth as a gravel driveway.

"Nothing is wrong with him," Agnes said from over my shoulder. "He's perfect. You, on the other hand, could use a tranquilizer dart to the head."

I wasn't going to argue.

Silas cracked a slight smile, the corners of his perfect mouth pulling up slightly. "Really, Poppy?" My name slid off his tongue smoothly, and I had to admit that I liked it. "You think that a detective gives away all his secrets to a beautiful woman just because she asks?"

Silas was also a huge flirt. I had seen him charm the pants off every woman he came into contact with, including my mother. I could only assume that he got around. He was charming and good-looking and again, had stable employment. If that wasn't every mother's wet dream, I don't know what was.

I just about swallowed my tongue when he shot me a wink that actually made me take a step back. Here's the extent of what I knew about Silas's magical abilities: he was a werewolf. You know? The person who turns into a potentially rabid wolf at a full moon. Paws, fur, and all.

"He called you beautiful. You should say 'thank you,'" Agnes hissed, her tone venomous. I was clearly blowing my chance with the handsome detective.

I opened my mouth to do just that, but instead, my brain short-circuited, and what came out was, "Did you know that werewolves tend to be more well-endowed than typical humans?"

Shoot. Me. Now.

Silas paused for a minute. Then he laughed. It was a loud, deep, and rich sound. Holy toenail fungus. He should do that more often.

My warm and fuzzy feelings at the sound of his laugh died when he smirked, "This is going to be a fun week together, Brains."

I opened my mouth to give a smart retort (or possibly a rundown of pensi size by magical creature type) but my words were cut off by a violent and ear-piercing scream.

4

Death Dust

IT WAS LIKE A switch flipped inside Silas. One second he was laid back and casual, and the next he was on high alert, ready for the unknown. The facade of the easy-going, good-time guy dropped like a cow in a tornado.

He was on the move before the scream had even stopped.

"Well, that's one way to divert his attention. At least he wasn't screaming in horror at your conversational skills," Agnes grumped in my ear. I paused for a split second before I took off after him, rounding the corner and following the sound of raised voices.

"Oh, my god! Oh, my god!" a woman's voice shrieked.

We rounded another corner that led out to the courtyard. Silas skidded to a halt, and I ran right into him. The man didn't even stagger, he was that strong and sturdy. I took a minute to admire his backside before I peered around his shoulder.

Three people stood around a pile of ash on the floor. A distinctly shaped pile of ash. "Are those ashes a body?" I asked, my voice catching in my throat. The words came out slightly garbled like I was talking around cotton balls.

"Oh, my god!" The woman standing over the body yelled. She was the one who had been causing most of the racket. Her voice was high-pitched and nasally. She was wearing a corsetted top and a flowing skirt in cream that highlighted her perfect figure. That, in addition to the cascading blonde hair, pale skin, and face dotted with an abundance of freckles, made her look like a Celtic queen come to life.

To her right stood a tall, blonde-haired, blue-eyed man with deeply pale skin. So pale in fact that he almost looked sickly. His face was sunken and gaunt, his eyes burrowing into his skin. His features were unremarkable, a jaw that was a little too soft, a nose that was a little too pointed. He wore an old-fashioned cravat with a high-necked suit. A little fancy, given the circumstances.

Combined, the two of them looked like they had just stepped out of a 1920s carriage.

"Mr. and Mrs. Dartmoth, I implore you, please take a step back," Darcy begged. A fine bead of sweat slowly slid down from his hairline.

I had heard of the Dartmoth family. They were a coven of vampires that resided in a commune up in the mountains. Once in a while, they would come down to stock up on supplies. But for the most part, they kept to themselves, preferring the company of other vampires.

Vampires were notoriously closed off to outsiders. My mother would often talk about the Dartmoths, citing their charity work and their contributions to her campaign, making it seem like they were pillars of the community. Other than that, I didn't know much about them.

"What happened?" Silas barked. His voice carried across the small space, echoing off the walls. The Dartmoths and Darcy looked up, alarmed.

"I-I-I just found him like this." Mrs. Dartmoth was in tears. They tracked down her beautiful face and dripped off her perfect chin. "I don't k-k-know what happened or who it is. Oh my goodness! Who do you think it is?"

"My dear," Mr. Dartmoth placed a placating hand on his wife's narrow spine. "You are in hysterics. You need to step away from the body before you have a fit. Please, my dear."

The burnt ashes of the body were lying in a person-like heap on the floor. As though whoever had died had been taking a nap flat on their back when they had been incinerated. Kind of like the statues at Pompeii.

I normally wasn't all that squeamish. I mean, as a witch, I've held frogs and watched large warts grow on inopportune parts of people's bodies. But something about a pile of ash and little bone fragments triggered an ever-so-slight gag reflex in me. And by slight, I mean, I wretched, loudly.

Maybe it was the fact that Silas was picking up a finger bone and the final joint disintegrated in his hand in a puff of ash. Or maybe it was the slight smell that the body gave off, which unfortunately smelled like BBQ. It caused a whole-body shudder and a second very large gagging sound to escape from my throat.

Silas's eyes flashed up to mine for a split second. "Don't throw up on the body," he snapped before he refocused his attention on the charred remains.

I backed away.

That honestly was the last thing that I needed to have happen. I had already dug a grave for myself with the "well-endowed" comment earlier. I didn't need to bury myself by throwing up on him and the dead body he was investigating.

"Who are all the guests in the house?" Silas barked over his shoulder to Darcy.

Darcy's normally placid face had gone ashen, which was probably a terrible turn of phrase, all things considered. He shook his head slightly and then sighed. "Yourself, Miss Seymour, Mr. and Mrs. Dartmoth, Miss Sabrina Cross, and Miss Lyra Nichols."

"And where are Miss Cross and Miss Nichols? Are they safe?"

"Well, I'm right here," a lyrical voice said from the corner of the courtyard. "I'm Lyra Nichols." We glanced around, and out of the shadows came a willowy woman. I was surprised at how well she had blended in with her surroundings. Especially given the fact that she had vivid ombre purple hair that cast a purple halo around her head. Her face was small and heart-shaped and her eyes were a soft lilac purple that matched her hair. They shimmered slightly in the dimming light of the courtyard, contrasting with her flawless dark skin.

The sun was beginning to set and the courtyard lights hadn't turned on just yet. Slight shadows were cast across the courtyard, making me uneasy in the gathering darkness.

Lyra Nichols stopped right next to me, her face calm and serene. She didn't appear to be bothered by the dead body-turned-ash-pile in the center of the courtyard. It was as if it had been a plant rather than a dead body.

"I also just spoke with Miss Sabrina on the phone," Darcy said with a rough shake of his head. "She was alive and well, and settling into her room. It's not her."

"And who are the staff members in the house?"

"I tend to the household," Darcy muttered, his voice gritty. "I am the one who greets the guests. We have a housekeeper who comes every morning, but she leaves around lunch, so it is well after her time. We also have a live-in, private chef who prepares all the food and then retires to his room. Mr. Goul likes to keep only a small group of close and trustworthy staff on hand. He believes that it helps to facilitate a more healthful, healing environment.

"And where is Mr. Goul now?"

"He should be in his study. He likes to prepare for each guest after they have arrived. And we...well, we had some unexpected arrivals, but he will be down for this evening's dinner. Mr. Goul," Darcy trailed off. "Well, Mr. Goul likes to make an entrance once everyone is seated."

"Well, I think I will make an entrance. Which way to his study?" Silas asked.

Darcy nodded, turning in the direction of the long hallway. "Right this way."

"I'm coming with," I said. I had no desire to be waiting around a dead body.

Mrs. Dartmoth, clearly, had the same idea as she also said, "Me too!"

"And me." Mr. Dartmoth chimed in, his arm still clamped around his wife's waist.

Lyra shrugged her shoulders. "Guess that means I'm stuck guarding the body until everyone gets back." She looked around. "I sure hope a breeze doesn't spring up and blow it away. That would be a little awkward." She laughed lightly, as though the whole thing was a joke. As though there wasn't a dead body that had been turned to charcoal right in the middle of the courtyard. Her comedic timing needed work.

I followed Silas, who followed behind Darcy, with the vampire duo bringing up the rear. And off we went. Strangers all walking around a strange house, trying to find the patriarch of the household. Because of a dead body.

We walked up the stairs and down a narrow hallway until we came to a set of double doors. The doors were large, reaching nearly to the ceiling, and were ornately carved with gold embossed handles and golden accents. Darcy raised a hand and knocked.

The sound echoed loudly through the silent hallway, like a foghorn on a misty day. "Mr. Goul," Darcy called. "There is an issue."

That was putting it mildly, in my opinion.

There was no answer from the room beyond.

"Mr. Goul, sir?" Darcy called again. He reached forward and twisted the handle, opening the door a crack. "Mr. Goul," Darcy said, sharper this time. "We are coming in. There's something that you need to know."

He flung the door open wide.

The room beyond was beautiful. With high ceilings and wall-to-wall bookcases. It was stunning. Like the library in Beauty and the Beast. The kind that made a book lover like me drool.

A large, carved wooden desk dominated the center of the room. Papers were spread out across its surface. A high-backed chair sat behind it, covered in what looked like red velvet. The room was completely empty.

"Mr. Goul?" Darcy looked perplexed, as he glanced around. He turned back to us, his heavy caterpillar-like brows pulled low over his face. "He's not here."

"Where could he have gone?" Silas asked. He looked just as confused as Darcy. Though on Silas confusion looked good.

"I-I-I don't know." Darcy's composure had slipped. The pristine mask of cool aloofness slipped. He looked scared and unsure. "Unless..." He whirled around. "No!" He hurried out of the room, nearly knocking into the Dartmoths on his way out. "No!" he shouted, as he ran past them.

I looked at the Dartmoths, then over to Silas who stood there looking as confused as I felt. Then he bolted out of the room after Darcy.

I made eye contact with Mrs. Dartmoth. "I guess we're going back downstairs," I said. I cringed slightly at my own words. I had never said that I was good at talking to strangers. Strangers in general tended to give me hives.

Mrs. Dartmoth's mouth turned up at the corners. "I guess so," she said, her voice smooth and calm now. "I'm Delilah and this is my husband, Sean."

"Nice to meet you I'm Poppy."

"Ah, the mayor's daughter."

I grimaced.

"It's never good to be identified as the daughter of your mother," Agnes snipped. "I'm sure she had some dark opinion of your mother. Wicked old hag."

I ignored her, mostly because it didn't do any good to answer Agnes in front of strangers. They didn't know me well enough yet for me to be talking to my familiar in front of them.

To Delilah, I simply jerked my head in acknowledgment, then followed Silas and Darcy back out of the room. With the amount of running around I was doing, I was sure to hit 10,000 steps here soon. I tried to glance surreptitiously down at my Fitbit watch to see. 8,157. Not too shabby.

I made it back down the stairs and into the courtyard in time to see what happened next.

Lyra was standing off to the side near the body, while Darcy was on his hands and knees, sorting frantically through the pile of ashes.

I cringed.

That was someone's body. It caused the same reaction in me that I had when we were spreading my grandfather's ashes and my mother had thrown them into the wind and ended up with a mouthful of ash. It's not like a piece of flesh, but it is still a cremated human. Human dust.

But Darcy was sorting through the ashes as though his life depended on it. Lyra looked unbothered but Silas had an expression on his face like he had swallowed a lemon.

"Why is he digging through that person?" Agnes asked in disgust. "That's disgraceful and disrespectful on a good day, and downright abhorrent on a bad day."

"I'm not sure," I whispered for her ears only.

"Does he know that was a person? He's not even wearing any gloves. Talk about unsanitary."

"No!" Darcy shouted from his position, his hands caked in ash. He held up something small and round. The ash had clung to it, making it impossible to see exactly what it was. All I could see was a large man holding up a tiny, soot-covered object. I squinted. It looked almost like a gold band of some kind. Maybe a ring?

"It's Garret!" Darcy gasped, tears streaming down his face. "It's Mr. Goul! He's dead!"

Well, shoot.

5

Magically Sealed Shut

THERE WAS UTTER SILENCE for a minute, then, "Excuse me, what?" Delilah blurted out. "Did you just say that the dead body is Mr. Goul? That Mr. Goul, that he...oh my!"

Darcy nodded, clutching the small item closer to his chest, tears leaving sparkling tracks down his ruddy face.

"The same Mr. Goul who invited us here?"

Darcy nodded again. He began to rock back and forth, whimpering softly. It was difficult to watch this big, bear of a man clutching his boss's possession and crying.

"How do you know?" Silas barked. His voice was sharp like a knife in the muted room. I reeled slightly at his commanding tone.

"Focus," Agnes hissed. "Need I remind you that there is a dead body, who could be the man who was going to solve all your problems? Don't get distracted by this one's sexy tone."

"My mind didn't even go there," I whispered back.

Silas shot me a funny look.

Oh, right. Normal people don't talk to thin air. But if I don't respond to Agnes, she tends to get more and more frustrated. And when she's frustrated she tends to start knocking things off walls and throwing things. It's like having an invisible cat that needs constant attention.

"His ring," Darcy whined. He held up the tiny thing that he had been cradling in his palms, wiping it on his pants in the process. I tried my best not to cringe. Dead person dust.

"This ring had been in his family for ages. It has his family crest on it, an eagle holding a wand. Mr. Goul is the last member of his family to wear it. He never takes it off."

"That's a weird family crest," Agnes muttered from beside me.

I couldn't help but agree. Whoever heard of a centuries-old family having a crest that involves a wand? Very rarely did people embrace their occult past. Not unless they wanted to be stoned to death or hung or lit on fire or drowned or pressed.

"Who could have done this?" Darcy's voice pitched higher at the end. "Who would want to kill Mr. Goul? All he ever did was help people. It was his life's mission. All he ever did was care about others!"

"Could it be a disgruntled former client?" Silas asked.

"The doors are locked," Darcy said strangely.

Silas looked perplexed. "That wasn't what I asked."

"I know what you said," Darcy snapped. "I am telling you the doors are locked. Not just locked with a lock but magically sealed. No one could get in or out. Mr. Goul oversees the sealing spell himself. No one can just waltz in. They have to be let in by myself or Mr. Goul before the spell."

"So, the only people who could have killed Mr. Goul?" I said slowly.

"Are in this house," Darcy said with grim acknowledgment.

"Oh dear. One of them is a murderer," Agnes sang with barely contained glee. "You're stuck in a house with a killer! It's like Clue but with real people."

"If the doors are sealed with a spell, how can we get out?" I asked the room at large.

"Oh, yes! That's a good point." Agnes chortled to my left. "A very good point. This just keeps getting better and better!"

Darcy turned to me. "We can't."

"I'm sorry?"

"The doors won't magically unseal for another four days. They automatically release. It keeps people from changing their minds when things get tough."

"So we are trapped in here for the next four days?" I asked, incredulity in my voice. Surely that wasn't right.

"You forgot to add that you're trapped in here with a killer. A murder most foul! One who just incinerated another human being without batting an eye," Agnes sang. "Oh, I can't wait until you get killed too. We can be ghosts together. Won't it be fun to have our whole after-lives together? We can haunt your mother."

I was 99% sure that she was being sarcastic. But who knew? Agnes seemed to live by the motto 'misery loves company.' So as long as she was making someone's life miserable, I don't think it mattered to her.

"No!" Delilas Dartmoth shouted. Her voice shrill. It bounced off the walls of the courtyard and echoed back. "Surely, we aren't trapped here! What if someone kills us next? What if they're a spree killer?" She cast a suspicious glance at Lyra's purple hair. "Some people don't seem to be concerned about a dead body in our midst."

Lyra for her part, looked unphased. "I like my meat a little rarer, Vampire. I would have thought you did as well. You should never overcook a steak. Besides, 'spree killer'?"

Delila sighed impatiently. "Spree killers are those who kill several people in short succession. They tend to not have a victim-type but kill fast for the fun of it."

Now, I love true crime as much as the next generic, white woman. It's soothing in a violent kind of way. But I don't think I would correct someone about what type of killer is currently hunting in the large murder mansion. "Surely, it's someone who didn't like Mr. Goul. Someone who had something against him," I reasoned.

"You're no fun," Agnes hissed. "Can't you just go with the spree killer angle for once? She did such a good job of explaining it too. Why do you have to spoil everything?"

"Mr. Goul had no enemies," Darcy insisted.

"And I have never met Mr. Goul before today." Delila was indignant, clearly upset with the subtle accusation. "I was sincerely hoping that he could help us with our problem, and I was hoping to be delighted by his company for the next few days." Her perfectly sculpted eyebrows narrowed at me. "Had you met Mr. Goul before tonight?"

"No!" I nearly shouted.

"Way to sound defensive," Agnes said. "Now, I know you haven't killed the man but yelling at people that you didn't makes you sound, as the kids say, 'sus.'" There was heavy sarcasm in her voice.

"I was also hoping for his help," I added lamely, ignoring Agnes.

"I don't think that anyone in this room knew Mr. Goul before tonight, other than me," Darcy said. "He likes...liked to keep to himself. His anonymity was important to him when going out and about in public spaces. He didn't want to be asked to perform miracles for people on the street."

"Maybe we are looking at this all wrong," Agnes whispered in my ear. "Maybe it was him. The butler."

"He's not a butler," I hissed through clenched teeth, keeping my voice low. Though, I swear that Silas's head tilted slightly at my whispered words.

"It's always the butler that does it," Agnes said. "Maybe he was disgruntled that Mr. Goul always asked him to shine his shoes. Maybe one day he snapped. He doused the shoes in lighter fluid and when Mr. Goul slid them on his feet he lit them ablaze. No one saw Mr. Goul when they arrived at the house."

"He's not a butler."

"Butlers are shady people. Who wears a suit in summer? He doesn't even look like he's sweating. I wouldn't trust a man who doesn't sweat."

"Good lord, would you shut it?"

"There's no need to be rude. I'm just trying to solve this mystery so you can sleep at night. You're welcome."

"Well, someone in this house killed him, and I'm not sticking around to wait and see if they decide to kill again. Give me my phone." Delilah had clearly decided that she was done.

Darcy shook his head. "The phones are also locked away."

There was a moment of silence.

"You've got to be kidding me!" Delilah burst out, stomping her foot like a petulant toddler. "Do you have a landline? Homing pigeons? Any way to get a message out?"

"Mr. Goul believes...believed in complete dedication to the process. We don't even use the internet when we have guests. Mr. Goul relies on his library to help him figure out the best solutions to his guests' problems." Darcy shook his head. "And I don't think anyone has had a landline since the early 2000s."

"I have a landline." Delilah snapped, affronted.

"Aren't you like over 200 years old or something?" Lyra asked, her purple hair bouncing over her shoulders. "That's practically new technology to you."

"Oh, bite me."

"You're the vampire. Isn't that your job?"

"So, we have no way out." Delilah was livid. "No way to communicate with the outside world and a killer on the loose? We have a werewolf detective, a witch secretary, two vampires, a cook, a butler, and a smart-ass. Great."

Lyra's face suddenly turned in my direction. "That's right! You're a witch, aren't you?"

6

Hello Chaos, My Old Friend

I FELT MY FACE getting hot all of a sudden. "Well, yeah, but..."

"You can do magic!" Lyra continued. "And the doors are sealed with magic. That means you could do magic to get us out!"

"Yes!" Delilah gasped in relief. "I had forgotten you're a witch. You can get us out."

I didn't know when she and Lyra had decided to team up but I can guarantee that I didn't appreciate it. I didn't like getting ganged up on and I sure felt like I was ganged up on now. "I am, but..."

"It's perfect!" Delilah said, clapping her hands like an excited two-year-old in a candy shop or at a petting zoo.

"Should you tell them? Or do you want me to?" Agnes asked, cackling.

"Look," I said, trying to keep my voice calm. "I don't think that's a good idea. My magic is a bit, unstable."

"That's putting it mildly," Agnes coughed. "Your magic is about as stable as TNT."

"What does that even mean?" Delilah asked. Her voice took on a snotty air.

I thought about how to best word my explanation. "It means that sometimes, when I cast spells, things can happen that, um, aren't particularly desirable."

But Delilah was too far gone to heed my warnings. She thought that I was the Simone Biles of magical spells. In truth, I was more of a T-Rex on a tightrope. I couldn't magic us out of this situation. Magic also didn't work like that anyway. You couldn't just fiddle with someone else's spells as if you were erasing letters on a chalkboard. Witches had used magic for centuries and we would still have people asking us to undo the magic of others.

"Spells don't work that way," I tried to explain. "It takes time and dedication to get the right spell. I also don't know what magic has been used to seal the door in the first place. It could be that it was a sealing spell. Or it could be a time warp spell. Or it could be a portal spell."

"It doesn't matter which one it is," Delilah snapped. "You have the ability to get us out of here. We are asking you to do so!"

"Well, she's unpleasant," Agnes hissed, her eyes trained on Delilah. "No wonder she contributes to your mother's election. They would be like two peas in a pod. Like peanut butter and jelly on a snobby sandwich."

I tried hard not to roll my eyes. Agnes wasn't wrong. Delilah didn't know about Agnes, but despite her prickly personality, Agnes had a protective streak in her when it came to people's interactions with me. She didn't like people trying to push me around. Or maybe she just wanted to bully me herself and didn't like it when others did it instead. I wasn't entirely sure. But Agnes had a nasty habit of haunting those who made me upset.

In middle school, when she had first arrived in my life, Agnes put a family of bats in the locker of my archnemesis. The girl was scraping bat guano off her books for weeks. Another time, in high school, she had slipped roasted crickets into a bag of peanut M&M's for another student to eat. The girl had only discovered what she was eating when one of her friends pointed out the cricket leg sticking out from between her front teeth.

Agnes was creative in her punishments, which is why I muttered quietly, "Don't."

Unfortunately, I wasn't quiet enough for bat ears because Delilah heard me. "Don't what? Don't ask you to use the magic that we all know you have? Don't ask you to help us get out of this mess? You're a witch and the daughter of our mayor. Surely you have the same drive to help people that your mother does. Or maybe..." She trailed off before striking out like a snake. "I might have to rethink our donation to your mother's reelection campaign. I'm sure the town would love to hear about how un-civic-minded our illustrious mayor's daughter is."

"Oh no, she won't!" Agnes growled. She sounded like a rabid pitbull and for a split second, I felt bad for Delilah. "That conniving wench! How dare she use that as bait! I'll show her. Actually, you should show her. You should hex her instead of unlocking the door! That would teach her!"

I didn't respond to Agnes. Instead, I forced a perky smile onto my face. "I can try. I'm just telling you, Delilah, you may not like the results."

Delilah gave a huff that clearly said she gave less than two figs about what I had to say. "Just do it."

I sighed, "Alrighty then." I tried to keep a spring in my step as I walked toward the heavy wooden doors. Maybe when this failed, I could take a bow.

Even from the inside, I could tell that the doors were enchanted. Magic leaves a mark around it. A type of glow that varies in color and brightness depending on the spell that was used. The door, much like the rest of the house was gold. It also gave off a faint golden glow, like an ember in a fireplace. That narrowed it down slightly in terms of what type of spell I was working with.

Glows of red, blue, green, and black tended to signify a darker type of magic, generally more hex or blood magic style. White, gold, silver, purple, and yellow were lighter forms of magic, the kind often seen in summonings, charms, and spells.

However, just because it wasn't dark magic didn't mean that it was easier to break. There are lots of different types of hexes. In a way, dark magic is easier to identify as the spells used to cast are much more specific. Light magic spells could mean anything.

I felt the rest of the cast and crew file in around me. I clearly was on display at a circus. Everyone was watching to see how to see how I was going to play this. What trick I was going to pull out of my sleeve. I just hoped I didn't light any of them on fire. Then I really would be a suspect.

I paused in front of the door. To anyone else, it might look like I was pausing for dramatic effect, getting ready to do a magic reveal and be the hero of the day. Get everyone out of the crazy-shaped house with its locked doors and incinerated owners. But in reality, I was gearing up for what could happen. Like a snake charmer watching the King Cobra for signs of a strike.

Odds are that I would make it a hundred times worse than it was before. I was the black sheep of the family, constantly doomed to cause strife. There was a reason why I wasn't trotted out at my mother's events.

"Ok," I said, out loud, rolling my shoulders back. Here goes nothing.

"I can't watch," Agnes said from beside me, covering her eyes. "Are they going to burst into flames? Are they going to turn to gold? Are they going to become camels? Who knows?"

I held my hands up and intoned:

> *"Like   water*
> *through a sieve,*
> *that nothing should*
> *ever block. Open*

this big old door,
hear   me,   and
unlock."

I waited.

Nothing happened.

The doors' glow didn't dim. The golden glow mocked me in its resoluteness. There was no clicking sound of the lock disengaging. There was no sound at all except for the faint tick-tock of the grandfather clock at the end of the hallway. No one spoke.

I sighed internally and repeated the spell—in my head this time—hoping for a reaction.

Still nothing.

There was utter silence behind me. The crowd realizing the full extent of my magical issues. I didn't want to face their pity.

"Uh, Poppy," Agnes said from beside me, speaking through her fingers.

Meow!

Some soft, furred creature was skimming along my legs, rubbing its whole body against my calf.

I glanced down, distracted.

A black cat was winding its way around my ankles, arching its back and purring loudly. I looked over and saw two golden cats, one gray cat, and a purple cat all sitting on the carpet staring at me, their eyes unblinking.

Hello, Chaos Magic. It's been a while.

7

Cat Acrobats

As far as companions go, the cats weren't too bad.

It had been a full thirty minutes with the cat brigade. The purple cat, which I assumed was Lyra, was gracefully jumping from stair to stair, its fluffy purple tail swishing playfully in the air. While Silas-Cat was still winding his way around my ankles. He seemed to think sticking close to me was the best situation. He also kept it up after I sat down. Gray Darcy-Cat had taken up a perch on top of the grandfather clock and was staring balefully down at me, judging me with his yellow eyes. Delilah-Cat was knocking the china off the shelf in a fit of outrage, but then calmed down and was now licking her paw in the corner. I had no idea where Sean-Cat had taken off to, but I assumed it was to get away from Delilah-Cat's turmoil. Smart feline.

I meanwhile was sitting with my back against the door. Hoping against hope that I could will it open with my mere presence. So far it hadn't worked all that well.

"Look on the bright side," Agnes said in a disdainful tone. Agnes hated cats with a passion that bordered on psychosis. One time when I had been looking at the shelter for a cat for company around my apartment, she had snuck into the shelter and released all the cats in the middle of the night. It had taken the entire police force a month to round them up. "At least the good-looking detective wants to be close to you. You haven't had a man who took this much interest in you in forever."

"He's a cat, Agnes."

"You're so picky sometimes."

"It's not being picky. It's being practical. If I wanted a cat, I would get an actual cat. Not a werewolf turned cat through Chaos magic."

"Again, beggars can't be choosers. At least in some form, he wants to be near you. He could hate you like the butler-cat." Agnes glared at Darcy-Cat. "I swear, even in cat form the man gives off bad energy."

I sighed. "I thought this whole ordeal was going to help. Like maybe Mr. Goul would be able to give me something to help with the Chaos magic and I could finally have a normal life." I shook my head with a scoff. "Now, not only is my magic going haywire for everyone here to see. But the man who could have helped me is dead. I'm going to be stuck with uncontrollable Chaos forever!"

Agnes sighed, heavily. "I understand, really I do."

I waited but she didn't say anything else. I waited some more before I blurted out. "That's it?"

Agnes gave me a side-eye worthy of its own meme. "Stop being such a bitter shrew."

"Seriously?"

"I told you I understood. I empathized! Isn't that what you've been wanting me to do this entire time? Isn't that what you're always harping on about?"

She raised her voice into a high falsetto. "'Agnes, you'd be more tolerable if you were kinder.' 'Agnes, stop being so mean and just listen to what I have to say.' Well, I did. And let me just tell you that you weren't saying anything new. You were just whining. Yet again. I get it. Your magic is like a magic eight-ball. The right answer is there somewhere but you have six other options that might happen at any given moment. Maybe try to look on the bright side once in a while instead of being Miss Debbie Downer."

"I turned everyone into cats!"

"And it shut that annoying Delilah up, didn't it? That's a bright side. She's not yakking at us right now, is she? She's not acting like she's all high and mighty now, is she?"

I glanced over at Delilah-Cat, who currently had her leg in the air and was licking her butt. The cat flashed me a look from above her butt, hissed, and went back to licking herself. I did prefer it to listening to her accusations.

"There isn't a bright side to everything though," I groaned. "What about last summer when Mr. Peabody asked me to put a spell on his pumpkin to help him win best in show at the fair and I turned the whole crop into potatoes?"

"He had the best stew at the county fair," Agnes said. "Those potatoes were hearty and filling. Again, you're looking at the wrong thing. You care too much about what other people think. Try to find the gift in your magic. Chaos magic isn't for everyone. Most people who wield it, die. You're still alive and thriving. You know, other than being stuck in a creepy mansion with a murderer."

She wasn't wrong on that account. Our family tree was littered with the ashes of Chaos wielders who had passed away young. Chaos magic is silly at its best and deadly at its worst. Those were two extremes that we always had to contend with. Most Chaos magic wielders died before 21. In our family, magic manifested after the eighteenth birthday and continued to get stronger the rest of your life. But with Chaos magic, it was different. Chaos magic was strong right out of the gate. It burned bright and it burned fast. If you weren't careful, it would swallow you whole.

A loud clink behind me made me turn. At first, I thought it was the door opening but then I realized that Darcy-Cat was playing with something. Something small and round. It rolled away from him as he batted at it, rolling toward us. Darcy-Cat chased after it. I stood up. The last thing I needed was for the cat to choke on a toy while in the thrall of Chaos magic. People weren't my favorite, but I liked animals.

I hurried down the hall and stamped my foot over the object right before Darcy-Cat's paws latched onto it. His claws scrabbled over the top of my shoe, digging in slightly to the top of my foot. "Bad Darcy," I hissed.

Darcy-Cat swatted at my ankle with a softer paw. I shook my head at him with a firm expression. Darcy-Cat then decided that the dust bunnies in the corner were more interesting for him than his long-lost toy. He scurried off. I bent down and retrieved the object from under my foot.

I realized with a start that it was the ring that Darcy had pulled from the ashes of Garret Goul's body. A shudder raced through me, raising the hairs on the backs of my arms. Dead person dust.

The ring was a burnished gold color. It was a singular, wide band, with the eagle—its wand clenched in its talons—front and center. I squinted. It looked like some Latin had been carved into the side. Since my Latin was a little rusty, I couldn't quite make it out. I brushed my hand over the letters, trying to see it better. The ring illuminated briefly in my hand, flashing a quick red color around the outside of the band. Then it was gone.

"What?" Agnes asked from over my shoulder. "You made a face like you were sucking on a lemon. What happened?"

I shook my head. "I thought I saw something. It's not important."

"Lemon cheeks, what did you see?"

"The ring glowed red."

Agnes came and stood over my shoulder, looking down at the gold ring in my palm. "Like fire magic red? Or like the eagle reflected the light and your contact prescription needs to be changed?"

I wasn't sure.

Agnes watched my face, then said, "I hate this house. I feel like it does weird things to my chakras."

"You're dead! Do your chakras even work?"

"Well, that's rude. Of course, they work. Just like a vibrator still works for me."

"Ew! Agnes!"

"What? I have needs. Just because I died doesn't mean that my desires did. Detective McHottie will probably star in my spank bank from here on out."

"Please stop saying spank bank. It weirds me out."

"You're such a prude. You need to get laid."

"The fact that you were 95 when you died and that was over 50 years ago, and yet you are still using words like 'laid' is a bit weird."

"I'm just trying to keep up with the times."

"The ring was red," I insisted. Desperate enough to change the subject.

Agnes let out a long sigh. "You're not going to let this go, are you?"

"The ring was red," I repeated, like a parrot lusting after crackers.

"Fine, let's say that you're right. The ring was red. That means that there is some fire magic, which occurs from a dark magic spell or demon possession. If Garret Goul was wearing a red glowing ring, then there was something else going on in this house. Something that we haven't been privy to."

"If he was killed," I said slowly, "because of a demon deal gone bad, then he had to have some sort of summoning circle in this house."

"Or it's one of the guests who summoned a demon," Agnes added.

There was one issue with that theory. Demons were notoriously difficult to summon and even more difficult to control. It's not as if you could just draw a pentagram and say some words that you had found on the Internet and then poof, you had your very own demon. Demons try very hard to hide. They don't like being called upon. Neither would you, honestly. If someone called you up and said "Now you're going to do my bidding because I said so," most people wouldn't take kindly to that.

Demons didn't either.

I had heard stories of demons purposefully misreading instructions and screwing over their summoner. They had a reputation for being malicious and reclusive.

I glanced down at the ring in my hand. It remained gold. Despite my insistence to Agnes, a trickle of doubt crept in. Maybe I was wrong. Maybe it was a trick of the light. I slid the ring into my pocket, intending to return it once the cats were no longer cats. It clearly meant the world to Darcy.

"Are you crazy?" Agnes practically squawked. "You don't take a demon-possessed ring and just put it in your pocket."

"I thought you said it wasn't demon-possessed."

"No, I said most likely you were imagining things. But most likely isn't certain. It's like picking up a rattlesnake from a zoo and hoping that it has been de-venomedized."

"I don't think that's the right word."

"And I don't think you're right in the head, so we're even!"

At that moment I heard a "What the hell?"

I glanced down the hall. It appeared that Silas had turned back into a human again. He was rubbing his bare chest in confusion and holy hell, he was naked.

Like buck naked.

Like I could see everything thing. Every slope, every muscle in his eight-pack (yes, eight), the very nice V in his hips, and...lower.

It was a new view, one that would be burned into my retinas for a while.

"See, Chaos magic isn't all bad," Agnes purred appreciatively.

"Why am I naked?" Silas sounded confused rather than alarmed. Like he was perplexed about his current situation.

But then again, he was a werewolf. Maybe they were always naked after a shift. His rough hands went to his hips and his head tilted to the side. A slight smile pulled at his lips as he observed me staring at him, slack-jawed. "Like what you see, little witch?"

A scream rocked the air as Delilah turned back. Her naked leg raised high into the air, her head licking her knee. Her cat form had clearly been ass-deep in tidying herself up. The scream had her lurching off the shelf that she had been sitting on and falling unceremoniously to the ground in a heap, her legs akimbo.

Darcy turned back. His big, naked bulk filled the space under the coat rack where his cat form had wedged itself. The coat rack tilted and then fell sideways, scattering coats everywhere.

Lyra changed back. She landed with grace on the back of the couch and then bounced to the ground, rolling to her feet in one lithe movement. Then she stood up, also naked.

She glanced around. At Silas who was still confused and perfectly naked. To Darcy who was trying to get himself out from under the pile of coats. To Delilah who was still screaming, trying to cover herself. Then to me, standing fully clothed at the end of the hallway. She smiled, and then in a light tone asked, "Well, did you get the door open?"

8

Moving Walls, Dusty Halls

To say that no one was happy with my Chaos Magic would have been an understatement. Well, I don't know if Silas and Lyra were unhappy with my magic, probably more perplexed by it.

Delilah was distinctly dissatisfied about being naked and made it known by huffing around the room before disappearing to find some clothes. Darcy gave me a disapproving look, one that was tempered by the fact that he was buck naked and obviously very cold. It's hard to look stern and put out when you're standing in the foyer in your birthday suit.

I had no idea where Sean was. I guess that he had managed to sneak off to some obscure corner before he discovered the loss of his clothes. I, on the other hand, had turned tail and hustled my butt up to my room as soon as I could. Not only was it awkward being the only fully dressed being, but it also was difficult to hide my embarrassment. Everyone in the room now knew the reason why I had needed to see Garret Goul.

"Do you think I can hide in here for the next four days until the door opens on its own?" I was face down in my pillow, having changed from my cute black cocktail dress into my pjs, a pair of cotton shorts and a T-shirt. It wasn't exactly the cutest thing that I owned but it was comfy, and right now comfort was essential. I had pulled my hair up behind my head into a messy ponytail, and it flopped across the pillow above me like a sad fish.

"Well, you'll be easier for the killer to target if he or she knows where you're at," Agnes said from her position at the foot of the bed. She was locking and unlocking the door with her mind. The heavy click, click of the lock turning grated on my already frayed nerves.

"Maybe if you stopped unlocking the doors, no one would get in."

Agnes paused. "Would you prefer I levitated the bed?"

"No."

"You're so picky! That's the problem with you. Fine, I won't make the bed levitate and I'll stop unlocking the locks. But if you expect me to stay trapped in a room with you for the next four days or however long you want to wallow, you need to give me something to do. I don't tolerate boredom, I might have to kill you myself—just for entertainment."

I snorted. "You can't kill me. You've tried that one."

"Clearly not hard enough. You're still here."

I glanced around the room, my eyes focusing on the heavy wooden wardrobe at the opposite end. "Move that across the room," I instructed. "But be careful not to mess with the floors. The last thing I need is a bill for scuffed hardwoods."

Agnes rolled her eyes, "Heaven forbid the floors get scuffed," she said. "There's a whole burned-up dead body downstairs, and you're worried about the cleaning bill?"

"What do you think they did with him?" I asked.

Agnes shrugged and focused her attention on the wardrobe. "I sure hope they at least covered him. The rain would wash him away or the wind could blow, and I'm sure someone wants his body so they can have a funeral." The wardrobe lifted into the air about an inch and slowly started to creep its way to the left, bypassing the bed. "I don't know how you would get him off the ground though. Do you think they should sweep him up? What if they got other bits and bobs with it? I would hate to be the person who had that job."

The wardrobe shifted to the left another few inches. "Who do you think did it?" I asked reclining back on the bed.

"I don't like Delilah," Agnes said.

I glanced over at her. Her brow was furrowed as she concentrated on the wardrobe. "That's a different question than the one I asked," I muttered.

"They both have the same answer."

The wardrobe shifted again, Agnes had nearly moved it a foot from its original position.

I screamed.

The wardrobe hit the ground with a thunderous crash. "What in the devil's bare backside?" Agnes was aghast. "Why did you scream? Is the murderer here? Is someone sneaking up on you?"

"Agnes," I pointed toward the space where the wardrobe had been. A dark sliver had appeared in the wall—just a small slice of darkness that stood in stark contrast to the lighter-colored walls. Beyond the opening, it was pitch black. "Is that a tunnel?"

Agnes sighed theatrically. "I sure hope not. This house would be a whole lot creepier if there were secret passageways behind wardrobes."

"Move it to the side, so I can see."

"OK, but are you going to scream at me again? I didn't like that, you know. I nearly wet my pants. My bladder isn't what it used to be."

"Agnes, you're dead. You don't have a bladder."

"That's a rude thing to say. How would you like it if someone said you didn't have a bladder, and just dismissed your issues like that?"

"I do have one. I'm alive." I said shaking my head. Sometimes conversing with Agnes was like having your head held underwater for a while, then resurfacing. I swear it scrambled my brain to talk with her. "That's not the point," I continued. "The point is a creepy tunnel in the middle of my room."

"To be fair, it was hidden by the wardrobe."

"Agnes, just move the damn wardrobe."

"Fine. But next time, ask nicely." Agnes lifted the whole wardrobe off the ground and slid it two feet in a few seconds. Part of me wanted to be impressed, but part of me wondered why she'd moved it so slowly last time. Like a magician's reveal at the end of a trick.

Behind the wardrobe, the blackness stretched wide like a mouth, big enough for a person to slide inside. The ceiling was low, creating a claustrophobic coffinlike feel.

"Well, that's nice. Now let's go to bed," Agnes chirped. The wardrobe lifted and started to move back to its original position.

"Are you kidding me? There is no way that I could go to sleep now, knowing that is there. We have to follow it to find out where it leads," I insisted.

"That sounds like a supremely bad idea," Agnes scolded. "One of the worst ones you've had, in fact. And I have been with you when you once had the bright idea to sell candles at the fire department fundraiser. You nearly tripled their business."

"Look," I said, brushing past that particular problem. "I can't sleep in here when I know that someone could be sneaking up that passageway toward me. We have to know where it goes."

"And what if it leads somewhere worse? Like a dungeon or a burial chamber? You won't be able to sleep then either."

"But at least I'll know."

"Your logic is astonishingly flawed at times," Agnes snipped at me. "Alright. Let's say that I indulge this wild idea. It's a dark tunnel. How will we see?"

"I'm sure there's a light somewhere around here," I muttered, feeling along the dark wall.

As though the house had heard me, torches lit themselves along the walls, illuminating the tunnel.

"I don't know about you," Agnes whispered. "But I think it's freaky that the house seems to be listening when you talk. That's some weird possessed behavior right there."

"The house is just being polite," I said, wincing internally because it was a stupid thing to say. The house was an inanimate object. It wasn't polite. Unless it was possessed. Then the house might be luring me to my death. Like a fly getting too close to a Venus fly trap.

Agnes smirked. "Ok, you go first."

"You're dead," I reasoned. "Can't you go ahead and let me know the coast is clear."

"No. Exploring the creepy tunnel in the murder house was your idea. I am certainly not going to help you feel better. Besides, as we've established, my bladder control is lacking."

"I don't feel like that's an excuse," I mumbled as I approached the entrance of the stone tunnel. The damp rocks stood in sharp contrast to the wood and plaster of the rest of the house. It also sloped slightly downward, like a ramp. I wondered vaguely how the tunnel system stayed hidden. It seemed impossible, given the proportions of the tunnel, that no one would notice the large amount of space it would take to conceal it. The house was certainly living up to its mystique.

"Garret Goul probably put this wardrobe here to hide the entrance of the tunnel from his guests."

"Duh," Agnes was examining her fingernails. "I think it's creepy. Having a tunnel into one of the guest rooms. I wonder how many other rooms have this freaky tunnel, or are we just special?"

It did beg the question. There were literally over a hundred rooms in this house, why put someone in the room with the tunnel? Unless you had something nefarious in mind.

I started down the tunnel. My footsteps echoed off the walls, my body casting large shadows that looked like ghosts moving down the halls. Down, down the tunnel went, gradually sloping more steeply until it leveled off at the bottom. At the end of the tunnel, I could see a large piece of wood covering what appeared to be an opening in the stone.

"It's blocked," Agnes said, feigning disappointment. "I guess Mr. Goul isn't as creepy as I'd originally thought. Shame, things could have been a lot more interesting."

As I approached the end of the tunnel to examine the wood, I noticed a patch of stone that looked out of place compared to the rest. It was on the left side of the wall and tapered to a blunt point. I touched it and felt a slight give under my fingertips.

"This stone moves," I muttered. I pushed harder and the piece of wood opened outward with an ominous creak.

"Scratch that," Agnes muttered. "It's still creepy."

I stuck my head through the crack in the wooden door and looked around.

The tunnel opened into Garret Goul's office.

The lights were low. Only an old oil lamp on the desk burned. The rest of the room was swathed in darkness. I stepped further into the room, hesitating on the threshold.

Nothing moved. Even the flame in the lamp seemed to be standing still. "Since we're here," Agnes said, "maybe we can search for some clues."

"OK, Fred," I muttered. Agnes looked at me as though I had lost my mind. "From Scooby Doo," I elaborated. "A kids' show." Agnes still looked blank. "Fred always said, 'Let's split up and search for clues.'"

"Considering I'm stuck with you, I don't think splitting up is going to happen."

I rolled my eyes. It didn't pay to have a ghost who was so literal. "You look at the bookshelves and I'll look over his desk."

I crept further into the room. With each step I took, I tried to lighten my feet. Yet the floorboards still creaked under my weight. "Could you be any louder?" Agnes griped from her position over by the bookshelf.

"It's not like I'm trying to," I snorted at her. "I, unlike you, am not a ghost. My steps are going to be heavier."

"You're not a ghost, yet," Agnes snipped me. "Let me remind you that there is still a murderer on the loose in this house, and here we are creeping around the victim's office after coming through a tunnel from your bedroom. You could still die."

Her words weren't comforting, and, knowing Agnes, they weren't meant to be. I had to admit that I'd had smarter ideas in my life.

I walked over to the desk and began rifling through the mountain of papers sitting on it. Garret Goul was immaculate in his housekeeping, with his bookshelves organized by color (wholly impractical if you asked me, but the effect was dramatic). But his desk was another matter entirely. Papers were strewn about, as though someone had been rifling through them trying to find a specific something.

"Do these papers look funny to you?" I asked, gently lifting a paper in my hands.

Agnes let out a gusty sigh and sidled closer. "It looks like Mr. Goul was someone who liked to read the newspaper and print out articles. Why print them out if they're online?" She eyed me shrewdly. "Is that what you were talking about?"

"It's more like the rest of the office is organized and his desk is in shambles."

"So? His housekeeper probably cleans the rest of the office and his desk is his own space."

"Or someone was looking for something."

"This isn't an Agatha Christie novel."

"No, it's not. But look at these articles." I held one up. One was about the Dartmoths and their philanthropic work. Another was a picture of the police officers. I could see Silas's handsome face staring out at me from the middle. "It looks like he was researching everyone."

"Again, that's not necessarily weird if he was thinking about the people he wanted to invite, he would have to research them."

I cast a cursory glance over the articles. "There's nothing in here that would lead you to think that any of the subjects even had a magical issue. Silas isn't mentioned in the articles. It's just his picture." It didn't explain how Mr. Goul had known about our various maladies. "There's got to be a notebook or something here somewhere with his notes," I muttered. "He has to have a journal or something."

"Why don't we wake up the detective?" Agnes was distracted looking at the bookshelves. "This is his literal job. He would be much better at finding a journal than we would be. This man," she commented raising a ghostly hand to gesture at the shelves, "has terrible taste in books. It's like he took a class in the most boring things to have on your shelves. He has classics mixed with magical awareness books. *The ABCs of Simple Spells: From Amazed and Befuddled to Yearning and Zealous*, for example. Or this one, *The Ire of the Demon: A Chronicle of Demon Possessions in the Late 18th Century*. Oh my goodness, I've seen this one on your mother's shelf, *Aura: How Simple Things Can Impact Your Mood and Abilities*. If that's what he's reading, I bet his program wasn't that successful. These are just hack books. I just can't even begin..."

I tuned Agnes out and went back to searching the desk. There had to be something. Some clue as to why Garret Goul had decided on the lot of us.

And someone he had sent an invitation to had wanted him dead. There must have been a reason why. Had Garret Goul known that he was inviting his own killer into his home? Had he welcomed them in?

I didn't hear the creak of the floorboards behind me. I didn't feel the rustle of air. But I sure felt the arm that wrapped around my waist and the hand that covered my mouth. I couldn't even scream.

9

Keyholes and Cops

I'M NOT GOING TO lie. I panicked. Wouldn't you? Someone had grabbed me around the waist, covering my mouth at the same time. All I could think was that the person who had murdered Garret Goul had found me snooping and was set to finish me off. But, I sure wasn't going to go down easy.

I threw my elbow back and heard a harsh grunt. But their grip didn't loosen, if anything their hand clamped harder over my mouth. "Stop squirming" a deep, rough voice said in my ear. "It's Silas." His breath rushed against the shell of my ear. I calmed slightly.

It was counterintuitive because for all I knew Silas could be the murderer. He certainly had the skills and wherewithal as a detective to get away with the crime. And he also could go unnoticed as a cop, by pretending to solve the crime. Stranger things had happened.

As he felt my body relax, he released his hold, allowing me to step away. I shot a pointed look toward Agnes who just stood by the bookcase with a sour expression on her face. "If that's how you react when a man grabs you," she scolded. "It's no wonder that you haven't bedded anyone recently. Men don't like when women scream at them."

"Women don't like when men sneak up on them." I snapped, partly to Agnes and partly to Silas.

He had a slight smile curving his lips, at my words, the smile slipped from his face. "I'm sorry," he mumbled. "I figured that announcing myself would have also startled you. It wasn't my intention to scare you."

"What a gentleman," Agnes cooed.

The traitor.

She clearly didn't share my suspicions. Still, I couldn't get it out of my head. "What are you even doing up?" I challenged.

Silas blinked. It was clear that he was expecting the blubbering idiot that he had met in the dining hall. My mother had once compared me to a rattlesnake. There and present, minding my own business, trying to blend in with the background as much as possible. But when backed into a corner, I came out biting. I wasn't sure that it was the most flattering thing to compare your daughter to a rattlesnake, but it sure had served me well in my life. I didn't go down without a fight.

He recovered quickly, a smooth smile spreading across his features. "I'm a bit of a night owl."

"Yeah, I guess being a werewolf makes you more *active* at night." My words weren't meant to carry any innuendo, but of course, they did. Silas's eyebrows shot up at my words. "Not that way." I hurried to explain myself. "Just that I'm sure you get busy at night." Worse, way worse.

"It's like watching a trainwreck in slow motion," Agnes muttered. "I can't look away."

"What I mean to say is..." I watched Silas's face as he smiled, his cheeks revealing dimples on both sides. Oh, dear lord. "Shut up," I muttered to him.

"I didn't say anything." But if anything, the dimples deepened. "But you're right, werewolves tend to be busy at night, especially when the full moon is near."

"Do you have a calendar in your head that tells you when it's time to start acting more wolfy?"

Silas's smile deepened. "Sort of. All werewolves have times when we feel the moon's pull. We don't need a calendar. We can just tell. Our wolf gets closer to the surface and begins to pace around in our skin."

I didn't even like it when my toenails were too long. I couldn't imagine having another creature under my skin. What an alien feeling that must be.

I must have said the last part out loud since Silas nodded slightly. "It can be. My wolf is a little different so he tends to stay out of my way a bit more, but he does wake up at night in the days leading up to the full moon. As soon as the full moon wanes, he gets quiet again."

"When is the next full moon?" I asked. Being trapped in the house with a werewolf and a murderer—who might be one and the same—was a bit much. Especially since I had only heard horror stories about werewolves.

"Two days," Silas responded.

"What do you do on full moon days?"

"Usually, I go for a run with the pack. Running releases tension. But..."

"But you can't run here," I finished for him. "What are you going to do? Is your wolf going to be okay?"

Silas shrugged nonchalantly. "I'll be fine, and my wolf will be too. As I said, my wolf is unique."

I wanted to ask what on earth that meant, but Silas had already moved on. "Why are *you* here?" His eyes lit on the half-open bookcase that I had just come out of. "What is that?"

"There was a passageway behind the wardrobe in my room that led here. I decided to investigate further. I want to find out more about the motive behind Mr. Goul's murder."

Silas's eyebrows drew together. "You have some sort of detective license that I don't know about, Poppy?"

I blushed. "No, but I watch a lot of true crime and I know that's not the same but I also like mystery books and solving mysteries."

Silas was silent for a minute, his eyebrows raised, then he let out a long sigh. "Well, I don't have any backup here. I'll take all the help that I can get. What do you notice?"

I stared at him, my mouth agape. I couldn't believe that he was letting me join in. I probably shouldn't have been so excited about being a last-resort partner. But I loved staying alive. That was a big one.

"His bookshelves are organized by color," I began, "but his desk is a mess. His desk is where he spends the majority of his time. He researches the people he invites here, but it doesn't seem to be incredibly thorough unless he is keeping those notes somewhere else."

"Where do you think he would keep notes?"

"Probably in the desk. He wouldn't want them sitting out where they might be seen."

"Have you tried the desk?" Silas asked.

"Yeah, genius," Agnes snapped. "You spent so much time looking at the newspaper article with the handsome detective's face, you didn't even try to open the desk did you?"

I flushed, "No. I was just getting to that."

"*Sure*, you were," Agnes laughed from the corner.

Silas nodded. "Let's get to it then. You search the left side and I'll search the right."

The desk was massive. With two deep wooden drawers on either side and a pencil and pen drawer in the middle. You could practically fit an entire soccer team in the space designated for the chair. The front of the desk had a wooden panel across it so you couldn't see the legs of the occupant when they were seated.

I bent down and opened the massive drawer on the left side of the desk. The drawer was full to the brim, stuffed with papers and miscellaneous knickknacks. Paperclips were scattered throughout the drawer, and stamps and sticky notes clung to the sides like leaves on a tree. Like the top of the desk, the inside of the desk was disorganized and chaotic.

"Nothing, but a mess," Silas muttered from the other side of the desk. His head was bowed as he picked up and read through some papers. "Old tax forms. Some letters from someone called Simon. But there's nothing here that stands out. How he could find anything in the desk is beyond me!"

"He wouldn't have put a journal on his shelves. He would want it close by." At Silas's bemused look, I said "Studies have shown that people prefer keeping important items within reach. Could there be a hidden compartment in the desk?"

Silas cracked another smile. "Statistics, coupled with cheesy mystery solutions?" He leaned against the desk, showing off the muscles in his arms. "Okay, I'll bite, where would this strange hidden compartment be? The drawers are proportionally sized, there doesn't seem to be a false bottom in the one that I looked into. How about yours?"

"No," I admitted begrudgingly.

He was right. The drawers were the right size and shape and nothing seemed amiss. But there was something that niggled at the back of my mind. "Keyhole panel," I muttered, my brain clicking like a key in a lock.

10

The One Bed Trope, But It's a Desk

"EXCUSE ME?" SILAS ASKED, his eyes narrowing.

I shook my head. "The portion of the desk that closes it off along the front. It's called a keyhole panel. The Resolute Desk in the White House has one. It can swing open if needed, but it's mostly kept closed. If I were going to hide something it would be around the keyhole. It's not technically a drawer but the panel could obscure something behind it."

"You want to tell him how you know that little factoid about the Resolute Desk?" Agnes snipped. "You want to tell him that it's a combination of *National Treasure* and an eighth-grade trip to DC? There isn't space in your brain for people's names but that fact takes come right out."

But Silas looked impressed. "Let's try it." He bent down and crawled under the desk.

"Lordy-loo," Agnes whistled. "That, right there, is a great view."

I shot her a reproachful look, even though I also admired the view. The man could fill out a pair of jeans.

I heard him rattling the keyhole panel. "There is something behind here. The whole side moves on this thing. Let me see if I can..." he trailed off. Then I heard a slight snap, and finally a "There we go!"

Silas emerged from under the desk, bounding to his feet with vigor. "I got it!" He looked delighted. He was so gleeful to be holding a dusty-looking journal, that I almost made a quip about his life needing more excitement."

He set the journal on the desk. "Would you like to do the honors?" he gestured in an exaggerated bow.

The cover of the journal was a faded gray, with worn edges, and a light coat of dust that looked like it had soaked into the cover. I opened the journal gingerly. The pages were pristine and shockingly blank.

"Huh," Silas said, his smile fading. "Somehow, I thought it was going to be more exciting than that. Why would he hide a blank journal?"

I glanced down at the pages. Then I ran my fingers lightly over the first page. There were grooves, etched into the paper. The kind a pen would make. "It's written in invisible ink," I said. I turned to the next page and traced my fingers across it. I could make out the different swirls of letters under my fingertips but could discern no concrete words.

"Invisible ink? How are we supposed to read it then?" Silas looked deflated.

"Typically, there is something that will make the ink appear. It could be a code word or it could need to be read under a special light."

"Is there a spell that you could use to reveal the ink?"

I cast him a skeptical look. "I'm sorry, did you enjoy being a cat? Yes, there's a spell, but I wouldn't put it past me to turn you into a tree or something, or accidentally light the journal on fire."

"Do books typically light on fire around you?"

"No. But who knows with Chaos Magic? It could be anything."

"I didn't mind being a cat so much. It was a change of pace from being a canine. Cats can do more things than wolves can. Their climbing skills are pretty impressive."

"I'm not chancing it. The unknown makes my magic volatile. This is why I avoid doing magic. It's too risky for me!"

Silas assessed me with a critical eye. "That's why you were invited to Garret Goul's house. Because you wanted him to fix you?"

I raised my eyebrows. "Wouldn't you? If you were the only one in your family who had magic like mine, wouldn't you want to change it?"

"I don't think you should give up something that is in your nature, just because it doesn't always work the way you think it should."

"So why are you here, Detective Werewolf? Are you telling me that you are 100% satisfied with your power and that you don't want to change it? If so, you must have stumbled in by accident. Maybe tripped over the doorway and fell inside?"

"What I needed from Garret Goul wouldn't change what I fundamentally was at my core. It wouldn't change that I am a werewolf."

"But it would change something about it. Isn't that the same thing for me? I want to change something about myself, not the fact that I am a witch."

"Your power is something that makes you uniquely you. No one else has what you have. It makes you unique."

Silas looked so sincere in his words that I almost believed him. But who would want to live with magic such as mine? You never knew what you were getting.

"Easy for you to say," I grumbled. "You didn't one time give someone a potion thinking it was a love potion and have it end up being a hair growth potion."

"Is that what happened to Elias Mars? I thought he looked a bit like Sasquatch."

I glowered at him.

Silas barked out a laugh. "I think it fits his personality better."

"That's beside the point."

"I guess my point is, don't sell yourself short. Just because the magic you do isn't always what you want, doesn't mean that it's not valuable."

"How sweet," Agnes cooed from beside me, fluffing her hair dramatically. "It's like listening to a poet."

I wouldn't go that far.

Suddenly, Silas stiffened. His whole body went ramrod straight. I froze too. My fight or flight kicked into gear. "Someone's coming," he hissed. Silas grabbed my hand, pushing me to the floor sharply. "We have to hide." Silas wedged his large body under the desk, and, since he was holding my hand, he took me with him.

I strained my ears to hear something, anything. But no sound came. Was he hallucinating? "Are you sure?" I hissed.

"Shhh," Silas whispered, placing a large hand over my mouth.

My freaking lips tingled. Seriously? Did the man cover his hands in cinnamon or something? It was getting ridiculous. I had read way too many romance novels and I always thought that the "tingles" people got were metaphorical. But I guess not.

His other hand released my arm and he instead wrapped it around my waist and pulled me in closer to his side.

It was a tight squeeze under the desk, mostly because of Silas's bulk. He kept his hand at my waist and the other locked around my mouth. I was just about to bite him to get him to take his hand back when I heard it.

The slight thump of muffled feet.

My body stiffened and I huddled back toward Silas. His lips found my ear, "Stay very still. Don't say a word."

The door handle rattled, loud in the quiet room. Then it turned slowly, inching open.

The figure of a woman slid into the room dressed in a hooded sweatshirt and yoga pants. I couldn't make out who it was. I shifted forward, trying to get a better look.

Silas hauled me back further into his chest. "No," he hissed urgently.

The figure drew closer to the desk. Her steps were staggered and halting, as though they were having trouble staying on their feet. They got closer and closer, swaying rhythmically now.

When she reached the desk, she began hurriedly shuffling through the papers sitting on the desk, looking for something. Silas eased me back further into the darkness underneath the desk. At any point, I was sure the figure was going to look down and spot us, confident that we weren't hiding far enough back.

But clearly, we were more concealed than I thought because she saw nothing. Or she was just too absorbed in searching the desk to pay much attention.

"Where is it?" The voice was soft and smooth, and noticeably feminine. It didn't sound like Lyra's loud and rougher voice, and it wasn't Delilah's more polished drawl.

The woman let out a quieter, more muffled, "Shhh, no. Stay focused. Don't let them get you."

"Oh good." Agnes drawled from across the room. "A crazy lady, just what this house needs."

I strained to listen to the woman's voice. She was in the midst of having a conversation with herself, the words soft but coming in a steady stream. "He had to have hidden it here. He couldn't have just left it out. He had to have it. Why would he hide it? What did he have to hide? Leave me alone!"

The last words were shouted, bursting out like a dam breaking. I flinched and Silas's hand began stroking gently at my waist in an effort to calm me.

I tried to focus on the feel of his fingers brushing against my bare skin where my shirt had ridden up, but the woman was speaking again.

"Shoot. Got to go. Before they come. But I have to find it." She darted away from the desk toward the bookshelf and began examining it. "It's got to be here." Then her whole body straightened and she pivoted sharply on her heels and fled from the room, slamming the door behind her.

I sat still in stunned silence for a minute.

Who was that? What was she looking for? I could assume that she was searching for the journal. But how had she known that there was a journal? What did the journal have in it?

"I think she's gone," Silas whispered in my ear. His words tickled the side of my neck and I shivered slightly. "I think you can crawl out now," he whispered.

"Oh." Heat flooded my cheeks, and I scrambled out from under the desk. "Sorry."

Silas shrugged as he pulled himself to standing. "No skin off my nose being in close quarters with a beautiful woman."

I flushed even darker. "Who was that?" I asked, trying to divert the conversation. As was well established, I don't do well with good-looking men flirting with me.

Silas's face turned serious, a shadow passing across his features. "I think that was our first real suspect."

II

Do Ghosts Lose Bladder Control?

WHEN I GOT BACK to my room, my head was buzzing with questions. Who was that woman? Had she murdered Garret Goul?

It was then that I realized I had slipped the small journal Garret had written into my back pocket. I thought briefly about returning it to Silas, but since I didn't know which room he was in, I stayed put.

Instead, I opened up the journal and scanned the pages. I could feel the imprint of letters pushed into the paper with the firm head of a pen. I tried to distinguish the words—trying to read them like braille—but gave up.

"You know if you were good at spells, you might be able to figure out what it says," Agnes chimed in from her position on the windowsill.

"What about you?" I asked. "You're always harping on me about how I can't do the magic, but you were a witch. Do some magic."

"I'm dead."

"Yet you can pee yourself and move objects."

"That's different. Magic is for those in human form. Peeing is universal. You've never seen a horse do magic, but you have seen them pee. And as for moving objects, that's a poltergeist quality I'm rather proud of."

"Not the same thing."

"Pretty much."

I went to bed with my head filled with scrambled words and hooded women. No surprise I didn't sleep well.

The next morning dawned and when I washed my face, I noticed that my eyes were slightly bloodshot. I could probably keep all of Garret Goul's ashes in the bags under my eyes.

I made my way down to the Great Hall for breakfast. Garret Goul's remains were still in the courtyard, but someone had had the decency to cover them with a tarp and cordon them off.

When I entered the room, the Great Hall looked almost exactly the same as the night before. Except now the table was filled with breakfast foods: parfaits, a large egg and spinach quiche, piles and piles of breakfast pastries, donuts, bagels, croissants, delicious-looking banana bread, and muffins in various flavors. There were also plates of fruit, from very average-looking bananas to elegant dragon fruit.

I was surprised that housekeeping had kept up with everything in the wake of Mr. Goul's untimely murder. It seemed that serving breakfast should be lower down on the list of priorities. Not so, apparently.

I paused on the threshold. The only other person in the room was a woman. A woman with long, wavy blonde hair that reached down to her waist. Her skin was pale with her freckles across her face. Her nose was button-shaped and her eyes were perfectly symmetrical. I had seen so many different TikToks highlighting the need for symmetry that I could see immediately that her features were absolute perfection.

At the sound of my feet, she looked up. Bright purple eyes met mine and she blinked. Then she blinked again. "Hello," she said, her voice calm and melodic, but I recognized it instantly. It was the voice of the woman in the office. "My name is Sabrina Cross, and you are?"

I was stunned for a minute. Here was this perfectly gorgeous woman, who had sounded deranged in the office last night. She was also the woman who was the lead suspect in Garret Goul's incineration. At least in my mind. "Poppy." I croaked. I cleared my throat. "My name is Poppy Seymour."

"Seymour? As in the mayor?"

I faked a smile. "She's my mom."

Sabrina nodded slowly. "She's always seemed, er, lovely."

I laughed. "The hesitation makes it all the more convincing."

Sabrina laughed, and the sound was like wind chimes. "I don't mean any offense; she just isn't quite my type of person. She's always seemed a tad cold."

"Try being her daughter," I muttered.

If possible, Sabrina's smile grew even bigger. She had quickly judged me to be an ally. "It's hard to be the daughter who constantly disappoints, isn't it?"

I flopped into the nearest chair. "Tell me about it." I reached for the quiche, cut a quick slice, then grabbed a Bavarian cream-filled donut to wash it down.

Sabrina leaned forward. "My mother, at my graduation, stood up and told the entire party—which included my friends and family—that I had only passed high school because she had slept with the principal. She wasn't even drunk when she let that information slip. Dead, stone-cold sober."

I thought her use of the phrase "dead" was a little telling, but I forced out a laugh. "My mother hides me away from everyone because I can't do magic like the rest of them," I said.

"That seems like a waste of good talent. If nothing else, maybe your magic is just giving people what they need."

"Well, I turned everyone here into cats last night when trying to unlock the front door."

"See? It's just purrfect."

I laughed for real that time.

"But for real, is that why I saw a cat watching me from my bedroom door last night?"

"Probably," I said. I had no idea where Sean-Cat had gone, maybe it had been to Sabrina to find help. She clearly hadn't been affected by the chaos. It must have had a radius.

"I now regret asking it if 'the cat got its tongue'?"

I giggled.

At that moment the door swung open. Silas stood in the doorway, his hands on his lean hips. Sabrina's eyes widened as she took in his appearance.

Silas for his part didn't seem phased by Sabrina at all. His eyes narrowed in on her for a second before flicking to my face and softening.

"Good morning, Poppy." His voice was like honeyed whisky. I used to hate those descriptions in books since who the hell has heard of a voice sounding like Jack Daniels, but it was. It was a voice with a lot of power, deep yet smooth. His eyes flicked back to Sabrina and narrowed infinitesimally. "We haven't met." He held out a hand. "I'm Silas Banks."

Sabrina rose in a fluid movement and walked around the table to shake Silas's hand. "Sabrina Cross." She eyed him again. "You look familiar, Silas. Have we met before?"

Silas shrugged, "Probably, I work for the police department as a detective."

"Ohh, a man in uniform. You know all the ladies swoon for that, don't you?"

Silas turned his attention briefly back to me, "Do they? Huh. I'll have to keep that in mind."

Sabrina's eyes also flicked to me. "So," she said casually, "let's see some magic."

Silas backed away quickly.

I laughed. "Smart man." I flexed my fingers, power racing under my skin. "Okay, what do you want to see?" It felt like I had found a kindred spirit in Sabrina. An instant connection forged through terrible parenting.

Silas looked hesitant. "Are you sure it's safe? I didn't mind being a cat but, umm, I prefer being canine, not feline."

"Who knows? Maybe next time, you'll be a kangaroo."

"Ohh," Sabrina cooed, "I've heard they're tough. I could totally see you as a kangaroo." At Silas's horrified look, she let out a melodic laugh. "Can you put a donut on this plate?" She slid a shiny silver embossed plate across the smooth surface of the table.

I focused on the plate, raising a single hand. "Silver spoon and plate so clean, let a donut there be seen."

The donut flew off the table, hovered in mid-air, and then I felt a low rumbling. Slowly, and with tremendous effort, one of the silver knives ripped itself out of the quiche and flung itself at the donut. It slid effortlessly through the hole at the center of the donut, taking the whole chocolate and sprinkle-covered confection and pinning it—with a loud thunk—to the far wall.

The donut shuddered from the impact, losing some of its sprinkles. It was an arrow, hitting a bullseye.

There was utter silence. Then Sabrina stood and walked to the wall, taking the plate with her. She reached up a slim hand and attempted to wiggle the knife free, but it was stuck tight. Sabrina pulled again, but it looked like the knife was now going to be a permanent part of the wall décor.

Sabrina shrugged her delicate shoulders and gave up. "I didn't want that one anyway." She walked intentionally back to the table and picked up one of the maple bars that was sitting in a pile, taking a big bite out of it.

Silas also seemed to come unstuck when she sat down. "I did want the quiche, though. Is there another knife someone could pass me? Without magic."

And this was why I didn't do magic.

"What did I miss?" Agnes asked, appearing beside me with a flourish. I had left her up in the room because she was taking too much time getting ready. How a ghost could take longer than a living human to get ready was beyond me.

Agnes's eyes flicked to the knife, then back to me, then to the knife again. "Why must you insist on trying to use magic to do simple things? You could have thrown the knife at the wall yourself. You didn't need to ruin a perfectly good donut to make that happen."

I flopped into my seat with a sigh.

Sabrina eyed me and then reached over, patting my hand. "Hey, it's okay. We're all misfits here."

"That's why we're here to get fixed," I mumbled.

Sabrina's eyes went unfocused. One second she had seemed perfectly normal and the next she had straightened and her eyes had gone wild.

"Wait a second!" Agnes gasped. "That's the chick from last night, the one in Garret Goul's study! She's the main suspect? Why aren't we questioning her?"

"Sabrina," I asked tentatively, "are you okay?"

"Not that kind of question, you moron!" Agnes ranted. "The kind like 'Why are you going through a dead guy's belongings?' or maybe 'Don't you think it looks sus that you seem to know that he kept a journal?' or even 'Did you murder him because you're boinking like bunnies with the butler'?"

I didn't know where Agnes was getting her jargon from. I was pretty sure it was TikTok, and I made a mental note to keep my phone far away from her when we got back. She had a scrolling problem and I didn't need her picking up anything else.

"What?" Sabrina asked, her eyes finding my face. Her eyes were slightly unfocused. "What did you say?"

"I asked if you were okay." What was going on?

Sabrina looked to the side. "Do you hear that?" Then she jerked her head quickly to the other side. "What was that?"

"Sabrina," I said, standing up. "Do you need something?"

"I'll go get Darcy," Silas said, getting abruptly to his feet. He ran from the room.

"Sabrina," I repeated, "Can you look at me?" I reached out a hand and gently took her own back in mine. I was surprised at how icy cold it felt.

Just a few minutes before, it had been warm and reassuring when she'd touched me.

As my fingers took hold of her hand, Sabrina spasmed. A cry echoed from between her lips, a loud keening wail that seemed to come from deep inside her. The sound was like nails running down a frosted window. Her whole body doubled over as the howl rent the air. Her hands tightened into fists, her nails cutting into my palm as they clenched around my hand.

The scream continued on and on for what felt like an eternity, echoing off the walls, until I was pretty sure my eardrums were bleeding. From the corner of my eye, I saw Silas reenter the room with Lyra behind him and two shadowy shapes that I was pretty sure were the Dartmoths. None of them moved, stuck in place by the force of the scream. I tried to wrench my hand free but it was as though every muscle in my body was locked. Unable to move. It was like Sabrina's wail had petrified everyone in the room.

Finally, the screaming stopped, and Sabrina's body went limp, collapsing onto me. I barely had the strength to catch her before she hit the floor.

Sabrina's eyes were wild as they locked onto my face. Her mouth formed words but barely any sound was coming out. She was trying to tell me something. "Sabrina," I whispered weakly. "What is it?"

Sabrina tried again, raising her voice to a whisper that I had to strain to hear. "They're back."

"Who's back?"

"The voices. They've returned." Her eyes rolled back in her head, and she fainted.

12

Black-Sheep Banshee

I NORMALLY AVOID CRAZY like the plague.

It's nothing personal. I just have enough crazy in my own life to last a lifetime. Between Agnes and my magic, I am all crazied out. And since I can't escape either of those, I do my best not to add to the burden.

It's part of the reason I don't have a pet. With my luck, I would get the cat from hell.

So, it made no sense that I was sitting on the edge of Sabrina's bed, my hand planted comfortingly on her shoulder. Cue the crazy.

Sabrina looked pale. Her golden, glowing skin was shallow and sunken. It was like she had aged 40 years in the span of 20 minutes. I was pretty sure she'd also gotten smaller. The luster that had seemed to coat her skin like dust had faded.

We finally managed to get her back—half dragging, half carrying— to her room. Silas on the one side, doing most of the carrying, and me on the other, doing most of the dragging. But we had gotten her out past Lyra and the Dartmoths and back into her bed.

She now sat, curled up in a ball, a warm cup of tea, which Lyra had scrounged up, in her hands.

"You must think I'm nuts," Sabrina whispered, her voice quivering with each word.

"Yes," Agnes said from beside me. "I think you're crazier than a cuckoo in a canary's house."

"No," I lied. I could tell by the skeptical look on her face that she knew I was lying, so I amended. "Not crazy, I guess, but you seem to have a lot going on."

A wan smile stretched across Sabrina's lips. "You could say that again." She let out a loud sigh that blew her perfect bangs out from her face. "You know when you pass someone on the street and you notice that they have a nice hat on."

"What?" Agnes and I said the same word at the same time.

"Well, now, say that person, who you only saw once, dies a few days later," Sabrina said. "No big deal, right? I mean for you. They probably have someone who cares about them. But you didn't know them from Adam. You just liked the hat. No harm, no foul. You probably wouldn't even know that they'd died."

She shook her head. "For me, it matters. For me, if I notice someone and then they die, I hear them in my head. I hear their voice, their last moments, and it causes me to scream."

"I told you," Agnes hissed at me. "Nutty bananas."

I was confused, but Silas wasn't. "You're a banshee," he said flatly, his voice not betraying a hint of emotion.

Then it clicked. There are many different and unique members of the magical community. It's a wildly diverse group.

Obviously, there are some—like vampires, werewolves, and witches—whose antics are well documented. But banshees were niche. We called them wailers.

They were the screaming black sheep of the mythical creature world. They screamed, they cried, they wailed, and, perhaps worst of all, they symbolized death. In other words, they were utterly terrifying to everyone in the magical community.

Whereas my magic was loud and in your face, banshee magic was dark and chilling. It seeped into the world and was designed to cause unease. No one wanted to be friends with a banshee. Ever. They brought forth images of your own mortality, and not in a good way. More like the way watching a horror movie also brings out your fear of death.

"So, do you know when someone is going to die?"

"No," Sabrina hastily reassured me. "I don't have a crystal ball that tells me when someone will pass away. But I know when they have passed. I know when they take their last breath. I know when they won't come back. I hear them go."

"Creepy," Agnes whispered, her breath fanning my neck and making the baby hairs stand on end. "What does that even mean, exactly? Like does she hear a whoosh and then dead air? Get it? DEAD air."

"How do you hear them go?" I asked, carefully.

Sabrina winced. "If they get shot, I hear the gunfire. If someone is next to them, yelling at them in an ambulance to pull through, I hear it. I hear it all, their last moments, the good and the bad."

An uncomfortable silence met Sabrina's words. "So," I asked, "is it normal to hear everyone you meet?"

"No," Sabrina muttered. "It's abnormal, even for a banshee. And it had stopped for a while, after the first time I was here. Things were finally quiet in my head and..."

"Hold up." Silas interrupted. "You came here before? To Mischief Manor? As a guest?"

Sabrina nodded miserably. "A couple of months ago. I was invited to come and be a part of one of the first groups. It worked. I was so excited. The only voices in my head were my own again. It was glorious."

She hung her head. "And then they returned. They came back all at once. I called and called Mr. Goul, hoping to get a response, hoping that he would be able to help me. I got no response. I called and emailed, but I heard nothing. I got so desperate that I showed up on his doorstep. Darcy met me at the door yesterday. He could tell I was in bad shape, and he convinced Mr. Goul to let me come in and be a part of this group. This was before everyone showed up. Mr. Goul agreed, he said that something must have happened to warrant a refresher. I was so relieved, I went right up to my room and fell asleep."

"What did Mr. Goul do the first time to make the voices go away? How did he stop them?" Silas asked.

Sabrina shook her head vigorously, "To be honest, I don't remember what he did. The whole time I was here was a blur. I can't remember what happened."

"That's odd," Agnes muttered. "Is it weird to anyone else that she can't remember anything? Shouldn't she know since it was such a big turning point in her life?"

"It was like waking a from a dream," Sabrina continued. "Suddenly, all the voices that I had lived with my entire life, every moment of everyone's death that I had heard was gone. When they came back, I freaked out. But yesterday Mr. Goul put his hand on my shoulder and told me that everything would be okay."

I sat up straighter. "Garret Goul was alive when you got here?"

Sabrina looked confused. "Yes," she said, "alive and well. He walked me to my room. Didn't he do that for you?"

I shook my head. "No, Darcy did."

Sabrina shrugged. "Maybe he was trying to figure out how to help me again and he was too busy." She paused. "It was weird, though. I didn't wail for him when he died."

"You didn't hear him die?" Silas asked, on high alert.

"No." Sabrina shrugged again. "I guess there must have been just enough of the magical fix left in me to block that out of my brain. Or the house has some magical properties that keep the veil between life and death in place for me."

It was late afternoon by the time we left Sabrina's room. Between her fit and the ensuing interrogation, a whole day had passed. I was hungry, tired, and cranky. My head was spinning about a million miles per hour.

Garret Goul had been alive and well just a few short hours before our arrival. Somehow his magic had worn off Sabrina, leaving her vulnerable to the same problems she had experienced before she came to the manor. And she hadn't wailed for Garret Goul. Maybe because she wasn't there when it happened?

"Do you think she did it?" I asked Silas, as soon as we were at the end of the hall. In my Rolodex of mythical creatures, I didn't think that banshees had great hearing, so I wasn't overly concerned about her eavesdropping on our conversation.

Silas rubbed his eyes. He had not shaved in the morning so he was developing a sexy five o'clock shadow along his jawline. It made him look more rugged and wild, as though the wolf within him was manifesting through his facial hair. "I don't know," he said. "I think it's weird that she was hearing voices again. Yet, she didn't hear him die. And the voices bothered her enough that she felt compelled to return. She could have easily gotten frustrated with him for not being able to cure her. It's plausible that she could have killed him as a crime of passion."

"She's guilty!" Agnes shouted. "Arrest her! She heard voices again and she snapped. Case closed."

"Where do you go when you do that?" Silas asked suddenly.

"What?"

"Sometimes you get this far-off look on your face and you zone out. What are you thinking about?"

I winced. "I'm not thinking so much as having a conversation." At his confused look, I elaborated. "This is probably the wrong time to tell you this, but I also hear voices." I forced out a laugh, trying to lighten the moment.

"One," Agnes said, "You hear one voice and I was once a real person who was in your family. It's not 'hearing voices' if you only hear one."

"It's my familiar," I said, trying to gauge Silas's reaction. "She's the ghost of my Great Aunt Agnes."

"Be sure to tell the detective how beautiful I am and that I was single at the time of my death," Agnes demanded.

I worried my lip between my teeth. "She says to tell you that she's single."

A ghost of a smile flitted across Silas's lips. "Tell her I'm flattered, but I've already got my eye on someone."

"He means you," Agnes crooned. "I will let you have him if you promise that you will finagle it so that he walks around shirtless. See if you can flirt back with him. Without mentioning weird animal sex facts. It's not always endearing."

"What's she saying?" Silas grinned "Is it normal to have a ghost as a familiar?"

"No, but nothing is normal about my magic. Why should my familiar be normal? Agnes is both my biggest critic and my avenging angel rolled into one."

"I am not your biggest critic," Agnes snorted. "That would be your mother. And I wouldn't use the term 'avenge.' It makes it sound like what I do isn't justified. Everything I do has a purpose and intent behind it. I merely bring karma into the equation."

"She says she's karma," I repeated to Silas. "But Agnes is the reason why there are times when I space out. Talking to her can be a full-time job and when she wants to be heard, she doesn't let up until I acknowledge it." I glanced at him from beneath my lashes. "I don't usually tell people about Agnes."

"I get it. You don't want to draw more attention to yourself with a unique familiar."

I nodded. "My whole life I've been different. First with my magic, then with Agnes. It caused a lot of embarrassment for my coven and especially my mother. I had hoped that Garret Goul could fix it." I shrugged. "I guess I get where Sabrina is coming from. If I had a solution and suddenly that solution wasn't working I would probably be mad enough to kill."

"Did she kill him? Has she confessed?" Delilah's shrill voice sounded from behind us.

I whirled around. Delilah was standing in the middle of the hallway, a frilly shawl covering her arms. Sean's arm wrapped tightly around her shoulders. Lyra stood even further behind them. Her purple hair was slightly askew.

"No," I mumbled. "We don't have any evidence. I was just saying it offhand." A fact I regretted.

Delilah's blonde eyebrows narrowed. "There's an awful lot of people around here who seem to have a motive for killing Mr. Goul," Delilah snapped. "First there's the banshee, who has been here before. Then there's the weird fae." She cast a suspicious glance over her shoulder at Lyra. "There's the detective who no one would suspect. And then there's you..." Her eyes flicked back to my face. "The mayor's daughter who no one even knew existed, who has weird magic. How do we know it wasn't you trying to cast a spell and instead murdered Mr. Goul?"

"Why is the wicked blonde bloodsucker here?" Agnes growled. "Someone should remind her that in the grand scheme of things, it's typically the vampire who's the killer. Maybe she got so hungry that she couldn't resist taking a bite out of Mr. Goul. Maybe her creepy, quiet husband helped."

"It does no good playing guessing games," Silas said, coming to stand beside me, his body a firm wall of muscle that blocked me slightly from Delilah's gaze. "There is no evidence that points to anyone."

"Evidence, smevidence." Delilah snarled back. "It doesn't have to be perfect to tie it to someone. And something stinks in this hallway."

"Her perfume," Agnes quipped. "Must be to cover the stench of blood and death that she carries with her all the time."

"You can't accuse someone without proof," I insisted. "Our kind knows that better than anyone. We were hunted for centuries for being able to perform magic. We don't want to stoop to the level of those who tried to kill us."

"Sounds like something that someone who was guilty would say."

Suddenly a glass lightbulb that was hanging over Delilah's head sparked and shattered, sending hundreds of tiny shards of glass raining down over her head.

Delilah let out a scream that rivaled Sabrina's and ducked, covering her blonde head. I shot a dark look at Agnes, who was standing, looking smug with her hands on her hips.

"Don't you glare at me like that?" She snapped. "That woman took it too far. You'd think that in all her years she's done nothing above reproach? I highly doubt it." She glared at Delilah's blonde head. "I could have done much worse."

Delilah looked at me from under her shawl, with a sour expression on her face. "I'm going to be next, aren't I? Clearly, I've made the killer mad."

"I'm not the killer!" I insisted.

"I disagree."

"Old bulbs," said a deep voice from the shadows behind me.

I glanced over my shoulder to see Darcy standing there, in what looked to be a night dress. His tall frame made the material look incredibly frumpy and old-fashioned. The man even held a candle.

"What?" Delilah snapped.

"We have old bulbs here. They do that all the time. Mr. Goul has tried to replace them. They just keep shattering. I'm very sorry, Mrs. Dartmoth, for causing you any alarm. I will bring a cup of warm tea to your room. Otherwise, I would suggest that everyone adjourn to their rooms, as tempers are running very high at the moment." His tone brokered no argument. With a disgruntled sigh, Delilah stomped off, Sean trailing after her like a baby duckling.

Lyra shot a glare at Delilah's back, before nodding to me and walking off.

Silas looked at me. "I assume that wasn't you?" The unspoken question being that it was Agnes."

I shrugged. "It wasn't me."

"Like I said," Darcy drawled. "Old bulbs." He waved us toward the dining room. "Shall we all have a quick bite to eat?"

13

A Kiss of Darkness

"YOU SHOULDN'T HAVE MADE that bulb explode." I hissed at Agnes, the second the door to my room closed behind me. "Now, I look like even more guilty!"

"I could have done much worse," Agnes fumed. "Bullies need to be put in their place and should feel the fear inside them, and the trickle of pee down their leg from time to time."

I rolled my eyes, tired beyond belief but also still wired. "What do we do now?"

Agnes glared at me. "Go to bed like a normal person. Or do you need me to rub your feet and read you a bedtime story?"

"I need something to do." I glanced at the clock on my bedside table. "It's only seven. I can't go to bed yet."

"Why not? I'm tired and I'm not even affected by human emotions anymore."

"Agnes!"

"Fine! Why don't you read or something? Didn't you bring one of the trashy romance novels that you love?"

"No," I grumbled, fully aware that I was acting like a petulant child. "I didn't think I would have free time, and I didn't think that there would be a kibosh on cell phones either."

"A lack of planning on your part doesn't mean I should turn into a TV and entertain you."

I rolled my eyes at her. "Fine," she snapped. "Why don't you read Mr. Goul's journal? I'm sure that'll put you to sleep."

"It's a little hard to read in its current form, you know. Empty," I reminded her.

"Then why don't you figure out how to read it? Do some magic that won't cause harm to anyone in here, except the vampires."

"There has to be another way." Risking magic in an already tense environment wouldn't do.

"While you ponder that, I'm going to go lay down. Don't think too hard. Your brain might pop out your eyeballs."

"Pencils!"

Agnes looked at me funny. "Markers!"

"Agnes."

"Sorry, I thought we were naming writing utensils. Why are you shouting pencils at me with a crazy look on your face?"

"Do you remember using pencil lead to make a rubbing of a leaf when you were a kid?"

"I played with yarn as a child and one time sewed my finger to a doll I was trying to repair. I didn't do weird pencil art. I don't even think I had a pencil. Spells don't require writing."

You'd think that Agnes had been a poor urchin on the streets of London, rather than growing up in one of the biggest and most prosperous Covens in the United States.

"You take a piece of paper, put it over a coin or leaf and use the pencil to make a pretty picture of the object underneath." My voice had raised slightly. "What if I did that with the journal? The ink might not be visible, but the imprint of the words is there! Maybe I can read what Garret Goul was writing." Without having to risk doing a spell. That part went unsaid.

"That's…" Agnes paused. "Actually not a bad idea, if I'm being honest. You positive you came up with that on your own?"

I glared at her. "Help me find a pencil."

Agnes grumbled but helped me search the room. Luckily, inside the chest of drawers, we found a couple of golf-sized pencils.

"Who uses tiny pencils like this?" Agnes griped. "What a waste."

"They work just the same," I said eagerly. I picked up one and pulled the journal out of the bedside table where I had stashed it. Then I flopped down onto the bed and opened the journal.

The blank pages stared back at me, seeming to mock me. I began to color gently. I took my time, letting the pencil pass smoothly across the surface of the page. I went one line at a time. The first few lines remained stubbornly blank. I growled under my breath.

"Oh, well," Agnes sighed, "it was a good idea. Shame it didn't work out the way we wanted it to."

"Shhh," I insisted, my tongue between my teeth. I continued coloring slowly, pressing down on the pencil with each stroke.

Then, like magic, words began to appear. They were faded at first, then, as I pressed harder into the paper, they became more distinct.

"Property of Garret Goul. For confidentiality purposes, no part of this journal may be duplicated or shared with anyone."

"Well, smack my tush and call me a 'good girl!'" Agnes said. "Would you look at that? There are words in this journal!"

She sounded delighted.

I kept going.

The second page was dated six months prior to today and it read. "It is with distinct pleasure that I admit that my goal of becoming integrated into the community has happened. I have worked tirelessly over the years to ensure that I produce something I am proud of. These are my musings as I head into this next year. After the rousing success of my first group of subjects, I find myself ready to take on another bunch. They come to me with some of the biggest problems in the magical community and I alone am able to solve them. I don't ever seek to toot my own horn, but the service I provide is integral to the magical community. I have succeeded where others have failed."

"He sounds a little pompous," Agnes muttered. "A tad full of himself, if I do say so myself."

"Agnes," I reprimanded her. "It's not good to speak ill of the dead."

"You speak ill of me all the time."

I shook my head and continued coloring over the pages, reading aloud as I went.

"This year my goal is to expand. I want to spread my name and message as far and wide as I possibly can. I will stop at nothing to ensure that my name is one day synonymous with success. There will be a time, years from now, when others will seek to live up to my legacy. In order to do that I must push the boundaries of what I can do. I must find other ways to help more people in a shorter amount of time. I must do this for my legacy."

"It sounds a little culty," I said aloud.

"You think?" Agnes hissed.

A loud knock at the door made both of us jump. We had been so absorbed in the journal that the knock startled us both.

"If it's that twat Delilah, I am going to go Casper the Unfriendly Ghost on her skinny butt," Agnes hissed. Then she vanished.

Agnes was someone who couldn't stand being left out of anything. And she always wanted to be the first to know what was happening.

Sure enough, she popped back in a second later, her hand playing wildly with her hair. "It's the sexy detective," she cooed. "Hurry and open the door. No wait! We should make him wait. We shouldn't let him think we were waiting for him. But if we wait too long, he'll go back to his room. Oh boy, what's a girl to do?"

"Agnes, stop it."

"You know I can hear you right?" Silas's amused voice sounded from right outside the door. "I can only imagine what Agnes must be saying to get you to use that tone with her."

"Okay," Agnes fluffed her hair again. "I'm going to go. I'll wander around and see if I can mess with Delilah and her ugly duckling some more. You, however, need to entertain a gentleman caller. Don't be too weird. But don't be worried about being yourself. Just don't be yourself too much. It might scare him off. Also, don't be too loose, but also, don't be uptight. And for the love of all that is holy, don't tell him the bear fact."

"Agnes," I hissed. "Go!"

"I'm going. But report back. I want to know if he's as perfect as he seems." And with that, she vanished.

I took a minute to fluff my hair and walk over to the door. Then I took a deep breath and opened it. Silas stood on the threshold, his hands in the pockets of dark gray sweatpants. Lord have mercy, they hugged him in all the right places.

Silas looked amused. "What was Agnes saying?" His voice was teasing and the corners of his mouth were turned up.

His eyes took me in, and it was at that moment I realized that I had changed into my pajamas.

Since I usually ran too warm, I had opted for shorts and a baggy shirt. Not exactly cute or sexy, but I hadn't thought that I would be running into any good-looking, stable men at this thing either. But the shorts were short and the shirt was long and from a certain angle it looked like I wasn't wearing any pants. I huffed and tried to pull the shirt up slightly so that Silas didn't think I had spent time taking off my pants for him. I didn't want the poor man to think I was accosting him. That would be embarrassing.

His eyes flashed down to the skin of my legs and then walked their way back up again. I felt it run through every inch of my skin like a caress and my skin flushed in response.

"Couldn't sleep either?" Silas asked, his voice low.

"No," I said, and then it hit me. "But I figured out a way to read the journal!"

"Really?"

"Yeah!" I said, excited. "Come in and I'll show you." I practically grabbed his arm and hauled him inside. His muscles flexed under my touch and I immediately dropped his arm. What was I thinking, touching him? We were in the middle of a murder investigation.

"Now, it's not all the way finished, but I did get some of it done!" I guided him inside and picked up the journal from where I had discarded it on my bed, handing it over to him. "I used a pencil and colored over it so that the imprint of the words was able to be seen. That way, even though he seemed to be writing in some sort of invisible ink, the impression the pen left on the page is still readable."

"That's amazing!" Silas exclaimed. My insides warmed at his praise. With my mother, it was always biting comments, and with Agnes, it was sarcastic quips. And since my life revolved around the two of them, I had no life. I didn't have someone who heaped praise on me willy-nilly.

Silas took a few minutes to read what I had done, and by the time he had finished, he was frowning.

"He sounds a little pompous," I said.

"He sure does." Silas was quiet again, thoughtful, considering. "Don't you think it's weird that he seems so obsessed with making a name for himself?

I always thought that he was doing it because he wanted to help people. But in reading his private journal it looks like he was doing it for the prestige."

"I mean, is there anyone who does a good deed, just to do a good deed? It's like Joey said in *Friends*, there is no selfless good deed. Every good deed has some measure of selfishness."

"Yeah, I guess," Silas pondered. "But this seems like too much. Like he's trying to build a legacy. People like that will often go to extreme lengths to protect their reputation."

"Do you think that he could have been doing something he shouldn't have and that's what got him killed?"

"I don't know." Silas ran a hand through his hair, messing it up slightly.

It was only then that I noticed how close he was standing to me. I could smell the faint scent of shampoo wafting off him. He smelled crisp and clean. And his arm brushed against mine when he leaned in to look at the journal.

My eyes flicked up and held with his. He was staring right at me.

His eyes flicked down to my lips and back up again.

I could hear every beat of my heart. Every breath I took he seemed to get closer and closer still until his lips were a few scant inches from mine. "Can I kiss you?" he whispered. His breath fanned across my lips, and I could smell the minty freshness of his breath.

I leaned forward. "Yes." I was pretty sure that my breath wasn't nearly as minty fresh, but at that moment he didn't seem to care.

His lips brushed mine in a teasing caress, pillow soft and smooth. They lightly brushed my mouth again and I stepped forward, pressing my lips fully against his.

It felt like a dream come true. Like I had been waiting my whole life for his kiss.

I let out a little involuntary gasp, and Silas took advantage. He deepened the kiss, his hand slid up to cradle the back of my head, his other hand wrapped around my waist and pulled me closer so that I had to stand on my tiptoes to meet him with the kiss.

Silas's tongue lightly teased the seam of my mouth. His hand was warm and firm on the back of my head. Both my hands went to his chest, to the loose t-shirt that was there, and pulled him tighter against me. He wrapped his arm around me, making me feel safe and protected. His big body moved, walking me backward until I was pressed firmly against the wall, his large body caging mine, pressing against me in all the right places. My whole body was on fire. Too warm, like a live wire.

"Emergency!" Agnes shouted from right behind him.

I broke away from him, gasping for air.

He looked confused. "What?"

"Agnes," I growled, my voice coming out husky and angry. "What is the emergency?"

"I...I can't, you, you just need to come now!"

"What?"

"Come now!" Agnes shouted. At her shout, the door was ripped off its hinges and swung wide open. "Now! I get that your loins are about to be on fire or whatever, but this is important. Someone has been murdered!"

"What?" I gasped. "Who was murdered?"

"Let's go!" Agnes shouted, practically dancing in place.

"Murdered?" Silas released me, a fierce look on his face. "Agnes says that someone else has been killed? Lead the way!"

With that, Agnes was off out the door and down the corridor. I took off after her, sprinting as fast as I could down the hall.

We rounded the corner at a run, me right behind Agnes, and Silas right behind me. Then, as one, we froze. Laying on the floor in a pool of her own blood was Sabrina. Her blonde hair falling around her head like water. Her hands were crossed over her chest, and she looked peaceful. Except for the massive amount of blood beneath her. I couldn't see her chest moving, and from the grim sigh that Silas uttered behind me, I knew he couldn't hear her heartbeat.

Above her was a man, towering over her prone frame. When we had rounded the corner, he had been bent over her, his hands under her neck, supporting it, but when we got closer he straightened.

Sean Dartmoth looked up, his pale face ashen, his hands covered in bright red blood. "It's not what it looks like," he whispered.

14

Another Oddity

"It's not what it looks like? It's not what it looks like!"

I had never seen Agnes so stunned.

"He's a vampire, standing there with blood on his hands and a dead person at his feet, and he's insisting that it isn't what it looks like? Has he lost his mind? Or does he think we're that stupid?"

It appeared that Silas agreed with Agnes, even though he hadn't heard a word she said, because he barked, "Explain!"

I shuddered at his dark tone.

This was police detective Silas. It wasn't the Silas who I had just kissed, it was someone who thought he was staring at a murderer.

To be completely honest, I did too.

Sean shook his head. "I was trying to help her. I found her like this. She was just laying in all this blood. She...she has been dead for a while. She was cold when I found her!"

"Yet you tried to help her?"

"I didn't know what else to do. With Garret Goul's death and now her's, I didn't want to be seen as a murderer."

"What is going on here?" Delilah had arrived. With her hair pulled back in curlers, and a slathering of greenish goop on her face, she looked like she had stepped out of a movie about the 1950s housewife. You know the one, where the wife goes to bed after her husband and pretends to just wake up perfectly beautiful.

Behind her was Lyra, with her hair mussed and dressed in a dark purple pj set. She gawked at Sean. Then she spun toward Delilah. "You were seriously accusing everyone else of being the killer and instead you were shacking up with the murderer the whole time?" She sounded gleeful, as though this type of chaos was soothing something in her soul.

"I...I... No." Delilah was staring at her husband, her mouth open. She looked like she was about to catch a whole host of flies in it. She shook her head. "Sean can't."

"He's a vampire," Agnes muttered. "Of course, he could."

Delilah cleared her throat and spoke louder, "Sean didn't kill her." Her face was set in stubborn lines.

"Are you kidding me? He's a vampire who's got the victim's blood on his hands. He's been caught red-handed. Literally!" Lyra sounded incredulous. "Please don't be like one of those wives of serial killers who fluffs her hair and says, 'I don't understand how he hid it from me. We tell each other everything. I never suspected, even though he has a weird shed in the backyard that I'm not allowed to go into, and even though he sometimes buys weird things. I thought everyone's husband needed a hack saw, industrial strength garbage bags, and handcuffs.'"

"You know what? She's growing on me," Agnes said affectionately. "We could be friends."

"It wasn't Sean," Delilah insisted.

"Delusional," Agnes muttered.

"Mrs. Dartmoth," Silas began. "I will need to question your husband."

"No," Delilah doubled down. "Not without a lawyer present."

"Delilah," Sean sighed heavily. "It's ok. It's going to come out sooner or later."

"It's none of their business."

"It sure is now," Silas said, "We are in the middle of a murder investigation, and you pulled me away from something that I wanted to finish."

"He wanted to finish sucking your face off," Agnes chimed in.

"Gross," I hissed.

"Don't blame me for calling it like I see it."

"Sean Dartmoth, we will not be one of those stupid people who don't know enough to get a lawyer when questioned," Delilah insisted.

"Delilah." This time Sean's voice was a bit more steely.

"Ohh," Agnes cooed. "Interesting. Looks like he does have a spine after all. I was wondering how he stood up."

Sean continued, "These are not normal times. I don't want to be escorted out in handcuffs." He turned to Silas. "I don't drink blood."

"Sean!" Delilah gasped.

"What?"

Sean shook his head. "I have never been able to bite anyone or drink blood. That's why I'm here."

Silas looked at me. I stared back at him. He turned back to Sean. "Explain better, please."

Sean sighed. "I was turned into a vampire in 1868 in Scotland. My sire was Delilah's sire as well. I had fallen in love with Delilah and wanted to be with her forever. I didn't care that I would have to be a vampire to do it." He reached over and took Delilah's hand, squeezing it. "Right after I turned, I knew something was different. You see, I had been told about the all-consuming hunger that I would have as a vampire, but I didn't feel it for blood." Sean shook his head. "No, the thing I wanted—the thing that I craved—was vegetables."

"Vegetables?" I couldn't keep the word in my mouth.

"That's what he said," Agnes said. "But seriously? He's expecting us to believe that he was turned on by vegetables and not human blood?"

Sean nodded at me. "Yes, vegetables. I wanted them badly. I would see a tomato or a carrot and my mouth would fill with saliva and my fangs would elongate. I spent time trying to make myself more like other vampires. I drank human blood, and it always made me gag. I had to spit it out. Can you imagine? I tried to pretend it was tomato juice and that didn't help. By that time, Delilah knew something was wrong. She helped me hide it from the others in our coven, but news has a way of getting out, no matter how hard you try to keep it a secret." Sean sighed.

"We were kicked out of our coven, and sent to live on an entirely different continent." He looked directly at me. "What you said about how we have all faced persecution for being who we are, we get that. We've had that happen."

"So you came to Garret Goul to try and get him to help you with your," I paused, trying to find the right words, "vegetable problem."

Sean cracked a smile, flashing white and pointed teeth. "Once we heard about Garret Goul, we both knew that I had to come here. We knew that if there was ever a chance of leading a normal life together as vampires and not being kicked out of every coven we ever joined, we had to try and change who I am."

"Why change?" Lyra asked. "Why not just keep eating vegetables? You're not hurting anyone."

"Being different in the vampire world isn't acceptable," Sean shrugged. "Delilah has tried feeding off animals rather than humans, to be less of a monster, and even that is frowned upon. There is a certain type of vampire that is portrayed to the world and a vegetable-eating vampire doesn't fit that mold. It paints a target on both our backs."

"Like being a Chaos magic witch," I whispered.

Sean's eyes flashed back to me and he nodded slowly. "Yes," he said, "like being a Chaos witch."

"That explains why you're here." Silas said softly, "And why you insist you couldn't have killed Sabrina and wasn't interested in her blood." He turned to Delilah. "But why are you here?"

Delilah bristled. "*That* is none of your business."

"Delilah." Sean's voice was strained. "Just tell them the truth."

Delilah looked at her husband. With her gaze on him, I saw her soften slightly. When she looked back at us, she sighed. "Nothing. I'm not here for anything."

Silas blinked, "What?"

"I didn't want Sean to have to come here alone," she huffed. "I didn't want him to change a part of himself without me there. I wanted to support him. Changing him was never my plan, but it's what he wanted. And I wanted to be here to encourage him. So when Garret Goul invited him to come to the mansion, I asked if I could come along. At first, Mr. Goul said no. He was insistent that Sean come on his own, but we have spent over a 150 years together. I wasn't about to let him go it alone. So, I sent Mr. Goul money to allow me into the mansion."

At our stunned faces, she snorted, "Don't look so aghast. Bribes happen all the time. Money gets us what we want out of life. And we have been accumulating it for decades. Might as well use it to get our way on this one."

"So you bribed Mr. Goul to let you come here, just so you didn't have to stay alone? Where is your sense of independence?" Lyra asked.

Delilah glared at her. "Maybe you've never met someone, Fae, who makes you feel safe, but I have. We are partners, we don't ever go it alone."

"I think Lyra is right," Agnes said in my ear. "It does sound like a case of codependence to me."

I shrugged as inconspicuously as I could. Did it seem odd that in the over 150 years of being together, they didn't ever want to be apart? Yes. But at the same time, it was a little sweet. Or controlling on Delilah's part. I wasn't sure which.

"Fat lot of good it did us anyway," Delilah continued. "Garret Goul turned out to be a fraud and now here we are stuck in a house with a murderer, who has now killed twice."

There was a palpable silence at her words. Everyone seemed frozen. "What?" I stuttered.

"We are stuck with a murderer who..."

"No," I cut across her, ignoring the scathing look she gave me. "The other part. The part about Garret Goul being a fraud?"

Delilah scoffed, flipping her blonde hair back across her shoulders. "Of course, he was a fraud! We knew from the minute we got shown to our room."

I glanced at Silas, then to Lyra.

Both their mouths were open, staring in astonishment at Delilah. Since neither of them seemed to be in any position to say anything, I continued, "Explain, please." I didn't mean to have my voice come out high-pitched and breathless, but it was a shocking revelation.

"You seriously didn't know?"

"Does it look like anyone in this room knew?" Agnes sounded about as snide as I wanted to be. "Read the room, bloodsucker."

"No, I didn't know. How do you know?"

Delilah sighed, as though she were talking to a small child. "The second we got to our room, it became clear that we were being watched, listened to, and studied."

I thought back to the tunnel that had been blocked in my room. Looking at my face, Delilah nodded her head. "I can see that you found something in your room that made you question things as well. If it wasn't the tunnel behind the floor-length mirror, then it was the fact that the room was obviously bugged."

"Bugged?"

"Those little listening devices emit a high-pitched whine. It would be hard for you to hear that with your average hearing ability, but for us vampires, it's really easy to hear. The second we walked into our room, it was like listening to a teapot whistle. We could hear where it was coming from right away—like lamps are a unique place to hide bugs," Delilah paused. "If I had to hazard a guess, I would assume all our rooms were bugged. He was listening to everything we said."

"Just because someone bugs a room doesn't necessarily mean that they're phony," Lyra insisted. "It makes them a creep and a peeping Tom and a whole host of disgusting names. But, does it make them a fraud?"

Delilah rolled her eyes. "Do you seriously think that we just left it at finding the bugs? When someone is trying to learn my private business, I don't just let it slide. I went to confront Garret Goul. And that's when I overheard them arguing."

"Who arguing?"

"Goul and his butler."

"Darcy?"

"Yes, him. Garret Goul was telling him that it wasn't working as well. And Darcy was telling Garret Goul that he should just let it go."

"Let what go?" Silas asked.

"How should I know? I'm not the detective. But after he said that, Garret Goul said 'But then everyone will know that I've been lying about what we do here'." Delilah looked smug. "Then when I found out that Sabrina had been here before, when you mentioned it, everything fell into place. He was a fraud and whatever thing he had been doing before suddenly wasn't working. He was panicking. And someone killed him for his lies."

There was a heavy silence after Delilah finished her story. Each accusation she had hurled hung in the air like a cobweb. Each sentence uttered another fly trapped in the convoluted web.

"I think we need to talk to Darcy," Silas said into the void. "We need to find out what he knows."

15

Freaks and Flighty Fae

WE FOUND DARCY SITTING in the middle of the study. He looked worn. Like all the stress of the past few days had accumulated and settled into the bags under his eyes. His eyes themselves were red-rimmed and slightly bloodshot. We had left Sabrina in the hallway, under a soft blanket and guarded by Lyra. We would have to find a place to put her body at some point. The thought of her just lying there made my stomach churn in discomfort.

When he heard us coming, his head jerked up. "I knew you would come find me," he said. His voice held a resigned note to it, as though he had run a long race and was suddenly very weary.

"You argued with Mr. Goul in the hours before his death," Silas said. It wasn't a question, more of a statement.

"Yes."

That was it, one word. One word that somehow summed up everything Darcy was feeling. I could see it in his face. The sadness, the regret.

"Care to tell us what it was about?" I could hear the impatience in Silas's voice. Someone else had been murdered and Darcy was the next lead in a string of leads that all seemed to be tangled like a ball of yarn.

Darcy chanced a glance around the room, taking in every inch of the study—and us. "When I first started here, I had nothing. Mr. Goul didn't care that I didn't have any experience. He was generous enough to take me in any way. To give me a home." Darcy paused. "I owe, no, owed him so much. When he started his business, I was right by his side. He had good success at first. He was able to fix people's problems without strain. He was able to give them their lives back." Darcy sighed, "It was inspiring. But over time, more and more people wanted a piece of him. More and more people wanted to be a part of his program and he took on the strain of the world."

"Strain has a way of coming back around and causing harm," I whispered.

Darcy nodded sagely. "Yes, and it did. He grew more and more tired, and things started to fall through the cracks. He started to get temperamental and unhappy. He wasn't sleeping." Darcy swallowed. "I had seen this before and I couldn't let it happen to the man who had given me a home. I owed him my life!"

"It's always the butler who did it," Agnes hissed.

I shot her a look.

"What did you do?" Silas asked.

"I knew a guy who knew a guy. I got a ring for Mr. Goul, a ring with magical properties. Properties that made it so Mr. Goul could do more in the day. So he could stay up longer, be more productive with his time."

"So it wasn't a magical heirloom?" Silas stated.

"No, it was not."

"It was more like a magical Adderall."

"In essence, yes." Darcy shook his head, wringing his hands. "In hindsight, it wasn't my best idea. It just created a dependence on the ring. Mr. Goul started to feel like the effects were wearing off. It was causing him some stress."

He looked me dead in the eye. "That's why we argued. He was frustrated that it wasn't working anymore."

"The Dartmouth's claim that Garret Goul was a fraud," I said hesitantly. "That he put listening devices in their room and wasn't helping anyone. And, they're right. Sabrina mentioned that she'd been to the manor before. Received treatment before."

"She had been," Darcy admitted. "It was before the ring so some things were not working for Mr. Goul as they should. He was tired. That's why Sabrina's treatment didn't work."

"And the listening devices?"

"Paranoid people do odd things," Darcy said. "Mr. Goul was scared that someone was going to steal his methods and take them for themselves. When the Dartmoths insisted on paying their way in, he put devices in their room to make sure it wasn't a trap. He didn't trust them. As far as I am aware that was the only room he put the bugs into."

"Bugging rooms and recording conversations without the consent of the person is illegal," Silas said.

Darcy twisted his fingers together. "If it had been in the privacy of the Dartmoth's own home, yes I believe it would have been illegal. I told Mr. Goul that. But he insisted that since this was his own house and he had a reasonable cause, it was legal. Technically, they could have chosen a different room."

Silas shook his head.

I wasn't a lawyer, but it felt like we were arguing semantics. And in the end, the semantics of whether or not a bug was placed legally isn't what mattered. "What did Mr. Goul learn from those recordings?" I asked.

Darcy let his hands fall to his sides, his fingers shaking ever so slightly. "I don't know. There wasn't much that happened in the time between us placing the devices and..." Darcy swallowed, "and Mr. Goul's passing."

There was silence. The heavy kind, when you know that someone is grieving, and you have no idea what to say to them since it would just come across as insincere. I hadn't known or even met Garret Goul. To me, he was just a name on paper. A signature at the bottom of a page. But to Darcy, he had been a friend as well as a boss.

"So, the idea that Mr. Goul was a fraud?" I asked, quietly.

"Unfounded." Darcy shook his head, twisting his hands together again, a nervous habit that he couldn't seem to hide. "He wasn't perfect, and sometimes, like in poor Sabrina's case, he couldn't solve the problem entirely. But he was a good guy. He was always trying to do right by others. The ring just changed him."

***

"Do believe him?" I asked Silas, as we walked back toward my room. The sun was rising, making the stained glass at the end of the hallway shimmer. Reds and blues reflected across the floor. I generally didn't like stained glass, for it made a house appear haunted and not by ghosts like Agnes either. But in Garret Goul's house, it was a tragic sort of beautiful.

Silas sighed "I don't know. I haven't heard of anyone having the skills that Garret Goul possessed. So it wouldn't be hard to believe he was a fraud. But it would have meant tricking all the people who came before. Only powerful magic could do that. Darcy sure believes that he was a genuinely helpful person. It also doesn't get us any closer to solving his murder—or the murder of Sabrina."

"We've got vampires who don't drink blood, a banshee who was driven mad by the voices in her head, a witch who isn't able to pull off normal magic, and a werewolf who..." I trailed off. Waiting for Silas to fill in the blank.

He cracked a slight smile. "I'm sure you'll find out tonight. It's a full moon after all. For now, what you've got is a werewolf who's tired. We should get some rest."

"Rest? We've only been up all night," I joked.

Silas smiled wider at me. "Take a nap, Poppy, I'm sure we'll have more to do later."

I nodded and opened the door to my room. I paused on the threshold, watching Silas walk away. His jeans clung to the curves of his rear end and his shirt dipped across his back, highlighting his narrow waist and broad shoulders.

"That man has a mighty fine tush," Agnes said. "But of course you've noticed. You're standing in a puddle of your own drool."

I shook my head at her and walked into my room, slamming the door behind me. I brushed my teeth and climbed into bed.

But sleep was elusive. I drifted in and out of dreams about secret tunnels, little mechanical bugs that crawled into my ears and listened to my words. Silas was there, as was a cloud of ash, floating in the air. Darkness surrounded it until it filled my vision.

I woke with a start, sitting straight up in bed.

"I hate when you do that," Agnes griped from her position in the armchair across the room. "You sit up like a vampire coming out of their coffin. It's creepy."

"What about his room?"

"Are you going cuckoo for Cocoa Pops? Whose room?"

"Garret Goul's," I said, "We haven't even looked in his bedroom. Instead, we just assumed that because he kept his journal in the library, we had everything we needed. That the journal would uncover his secrets. But what about his room? What if he kept information in there that could point to what or who killed him?"

"You can't just sleep like a normal person. Your mind has to be going and then you wake up with these hair-brained ideas about exploring a dead man's room." Agnes huffed and pulled herself out of the chair. "Ok, I'll bite, let's go get the hot detective and search the crispy Mr. Goul's room."

I chewed on my bottom lip. Silas hadn't liked the logistics of illegal listening devices. He seemed as straight as an arrow when it came to the letter of the law. "He would want a warrant."

"Do you need a warrant to search a dead man's room?" Agnes asked.

"I don't know. I'm not a lawyer. But what if Silas does? Then we would have to wait, and the killer could be hiding evidence. Or if we wait, they could get away."

"So," Agnes muttered acerbically, "you're suggesting that we don't get the wolfman, and instead go into the room of the dead guy on our own?"

"We'll be together."

Agnes shot me a sour look. "Yes, that makes me feel so much better. Having you by my side is the exact same thing as having a six-foot-two muscle man. Why didn't I think of that?"

I stood and made my way out into the hallway, trying to be light on my feet. The whole house, despite the light filtering in through the windows and the warm, yet slightly stale air, felt off. Is a murderer waiting around any corner, ready to strike like a cornered snake?

I turned down the narrow hallway and into the wider and more spacious corridor. No one was around. I was all by myself, completely and utterly alone...

"Why are we sneaking?" The voice was right in my ear and was accompanied by a warm breath on my neck.

"Holy rattails!" I leaped into the air, coming down to face Lyra who stood maybe a foot away from me, her hands crossed over her chest. Her hair was a soft lavender purple, curled perfectly so it fell in beautiful waves over her shoulders. I kind of wondered how she was able to style it amid a murder investigation.

She chuckled. "Sorry, I didn't mean to scare you. I saw you sneaking around and was wondering if everything was okay?"

"I'm not sneaking," I said, defensively.

"You were sneaking," Agnes said dryly. "Poorly, but you were sneaking."

"Okay, then," Lyra said easily. "Why are you tiptoeing through the hallways?"

I debated, briefly, if I should tell her. "I want to see Garret Goul's room. I'm wondering if he left any evidence there or if something was out of place that I could spot."

Lyra's face was impassive for a minute, then she smiled broadly. "I knew I liked you. Let's go!"

"Let's go?"

"Hell, yeah! You think that I'm going to let you have all the fun? If there's something there, I want to know about it!"

"You want to know about it?"

Lyra looked confused. "Yes, wouldn't you? I'm a naturally nosey person. I like to be up in everyone's business." She winked at me. "Don't worry though, I don't tell other people's secrets. I just like knowing them myself."

"I can respect that," Agnes said. " Nosey is the only way. Let's go!"

I nodded at Lyra and the three of us set off down the corridor.

"Speaking of nosey," Lyra said, "what's with you and the detective?"

I looked over at her. I don't have many friends. The witches in my coven tend to steer clear of Chaos magic and I don't get out of the house much. Eyes are everywhere, waiting for me to mess up so they can report back to my mother. I felt like I was doing a disservice to my mother if I partied too hard. So, when Lyra asked me about Silas with her secretive "girl gossip" tone, I didn't know if it was a normal conversation between friends or if she was being nosey. I decided to lean into it.

"I don't know for sure," I said. "He's good-looking and we did share a kiss before we found Sabrina."

"Yes! I knew it! I knew there was chemistry there. I could see it in the way he looked at you! Was it good? Did he use too much tongue? He is a werewolf after all. They slobber in wolf form, so it would kill my fantasy if they did in human form as well."

"It was," I trailed off, trying to come up with the right words. I sighed. "It was the best kiss of my life. Granted, I haven't had all that many, but still."

"He's got great lips. It's a good thing that he knows how to use them," Lyra said.

We turned down another hallway, the winding path to Garret Goul's bedroom showing just how isolated his room was from the guests' quarters. At the end of the hallway were two giant, ten-foot, ornate gold doors, with large, lion-head knockers on each side. The doors looked like they belonged on the outside of the house but had been cut out and moved inside for dramatic effect. They were garish and over the top—two things that I had come to associate with Garret Goul.

"Do you think he had naughty sex parties in there?" Lyra suddenly asked. "The knockers are pretty brazen."

"Oh, this is going to be good," Agnes said, rubbing her hands together.

"What? The whole house screams naughty party to me. The doors, the gold, everything is over the top in a way that screams freaky nights between the sheets."

I froze. "Did you just respond to Agnes?"

16

The Cost of a Ring

Lyra glanced back at me, not at all aware that she'd just dropped a bombshell. "You mean your familiar? Yeah, she's snarky, I like it."

"No one ever sees Agnes."

Agnes had also stopped and was staring aghast at Lyra. "How can she see me? Is she a ghost too? Does she think my hair looks weird?"

"Nah," Lyra said, addressing Agnes directly. "I'm Fae. We can hear everything, even the supernatural. I can't see you, so you'd need to talk for me to know where you are positionally, but otherwise, I can hear every word you say."

"Good lord, even the stuff I said about the detective?"

Lyra grinned wickedly. "Don't worry, I won't tell him how much you ogle his butt."

"I don't ogle it that much," Agnes said defensively.

"Sure, you do, and why shouldn't you? You and my grandmother are very similar. She also likes to look at butts. Doesn't matter the gender either. She just likes looking at everyone's rear end. Taking her to the grocery store is a study in patience. It's a great opener though."

While Agnes stood with her mouth open, I was staring at Lyra. I had never met a Fae before. They keep to themselves, typically living on the edges of the forests. They didn't hold jobs in the city ever or at least not often.

"What exactly can Fae do?" I asked.

Lyra blinked, then a huge smile spread across her face. "No one has ever been that direct with me before." She waved a hand. "Let's see, Fae can sense energy. We are drawn to it. We can use that energy to manipulate our bodies into shapes. We can turn into another person or become small to fit through doors or large to move things out of the way."

"How do you get energy?"

"We get small amounts through food, but mostly from other people. It can make the other person tired when we steal energy, so we don't do it often, and never without permission."

"Can you put someone to sleep with it?" I asked, genuinely curious.

Lyra winced. "Yes, but no one knows if it's the energy draining or if Fae are just really dull."

"You don't seem dull to me."

"You've never been at a party with my Uncle Sal. That man could make watching paint dry seem like the Olympics."

"Like your mother," Agnes said. "That woman pisses my britches, and could put a sloth to sleep."

Lyra looked amused. "Is she always this outspoken?"

"Yes," Agnes and I said at the same time.

Lyra chuckled. She reached for the door handle. "Guess now is as good a time as any to go into the dead man's room."

"Should we knock?" I asked.

Both Lyra and Agnes raised their eyebrows at me in nearly identical expressions of confusion. "I think I would be more worried if someone answered the knock," Lyra said. "It's like that old question: 'If you heard a fart when you were sure you were alone in a room, would you laugh or cry?'"

I hadn't heard that one before, but I was positive I would cry. Sighing, I stepped forward. "Open it," I said.

Slowly Lyra twisted the handle, swinging the golden door open wide.

I didn't know what I expected. I guess after the opulence of the library and the Great Hall, I had expected Garret Goul's bedroom to be another over-the-top, outlandish room. It wasn't.

There was almost an absence of color. The walls were a dark red, so dark that it almost looked black. The bed was a wooden monstrosity that had also been painted black. The bedding was more dark red and the carpet was a plush-looking gray.

The walls were lined with paintings in gold frames, but that was the only color that stood out brightly in the room. The paintings were matte, with scenes depicting rainy skies and abstracts in grays and blacks. Against the far wall was a dresser and a door that I assumed led to a bathroom.

There weren't any personal touches around the room. No pictures of family members, not even books or papers scattered anywhere. The room was sterile and boring.

"This room is spooky," Lyra muttered.

"It looks like a sex dungeon, but without the kinky toys," Agnes muttered.

"I don't know," Lyra said. "We might be able to find some." She took a step back and looked around. "Those curtains look like they could have been used to tie someone up at one point."

"It's so weird that you respond to things that I say," Agnes marveled. "I'm only used to Poppy being able to hear me."

"I don't know," Lyra said, looking around, opening drawers and rustling the heavy curtains. "I kind of like being able to hear you. It's fun. It's like having the snarky voices inside your head on the outside and said through someone else."

"I'm not snarky."

"How many times have you called Delilah a name?"

"That's not snark. That's called being realistic and cognizant of others."

"My favorite was the comment about her perfume. I almost lost it that time."

"I don't say anything that isn't true," Agnes muttered. "I just don't sugarcoat things."

"I get it," Lyra responded. "You have to tell it like it is sometimes. Just most people don't." She opened another drawer. "Where are all this man's clothes? Like I know there's a stereotype of men not wearing different outfits. But seriously? He has nothing in the drawers. It's like he never even lived in this room."

"Are you rifling through his drawers?" I asked. It seemed a little bit insensitive to me, especially since we had found Garret Goul in a pile of ash mere days before. Besides, what if she found his underwear or something?

Lyra glanced up at me. "I'm sorry, but aren't we here to investigate? I want to look around. If you get squeamish about looking through a dead man's belongings, you should have just let me go in."

"I'm not squeamish about it. More like..." I paused, trying to think of what I wanted to say.

"Like...what?" Lyra shrugged. "It's ok to be squeamish about something like death. It's a freaky and unsettling thing. Like what happens when you die? I mean you have a ghost as a familiar, so you probably know better than me, but it's a question that haunts all of mankind."

"Psychology is bullshit," Agnes said. "I stopped listening when Freud told me that I secretly wanted a penis. Imagine riding a bike with that swinging between your legs."

"Look, I want to know how Goul died. His room might give us some clues. Or it will give us the absence of clues, which is a clue in and of itself." Lyra dropped to her knees and began looking under the dresser. Then she shuffled across the room on her knees to look under the bed. "So far, I've learned that Garret Goul didn't have any clothes in his drawers. He doesn't like clutter or personal things. He probably doesn't have a sex fetish since no juicy things are lying around. I don't see any ropes or hooks."

She reared back from under the bed as though stung. "And apparently, he needed protection."

17

Etched in Ash

"What?" Agnes shrieked. "Is it a knife? Writing in blood? Is it Garret Goul's head?"

"Wouldn't his head smell after a while if it were?" Lyra asked.

"Agnes was a librarian in her life, not a coroner. She has no training and currently no sense of smell," I replied. I knelt and crawled toward the footboard, peering under the base. There, carved in wood, was a symbol resembling a trident but with completely straight lines. "What is that?" I asked, scooting closer and wedging my body further under the bed to get a better look.

"It looks like someone took a knife and carved it there." Lyra crawled under the bed so that her whole body was wedged underneath it with just her feet hanging out. You had to admire the commitment. "There's one on this side too."

I army crawled forward to the headboard. "There's one up here, too."

"Why would he carve a symbol into his bed? It's the same one too, on all four corners."

"Let me see," Agnes barked. She vanished from view and then appeared, spread-eagled on her back beneath the bed. "That's the Norse rune of protection, Algiz. It symbolizes protection from external forces—typically otherworldly forces—and forces of evil or death. It is said to look like a raven claw to represent one of the ravens that Odin had on his shoulder."

"How on earth did you know that?" I asked, a little impressed.

"I might not have a sense of smell, but my eyesight works just fine. And as, you said, I was a librarian. I like to read books. Before the invention of the dirty books that I currently love, I did love history books. Viking and Greek mythology were incredibly important to me."

"What about the Romans?" Lyra asked.

Agnes rolled her eyes. "The Romans stole Greek mythology and changed the names. There isn't anything original there."

"My ancestors were Roman seers," Lyra deadpanned.

"My condolences," Agnes said. "We can't help who we are related to. I sure hope you can overcome that issue with your genetics just fine in the long run."

Lyra blinked, and then she burst out laughing. She laughed so hard that she hit her head on the bottom of the bed. She rolled out from under the bed, still laughing. "I like you, Agnes," she said. "You say what you mean, and mean what you say."

Agnes sniffed. "I don't know why you would ever beat around the bush. It does nothing but get leaves in your hair."

I pulled myself out from under the bed and Agnes vanished to rejoin us standing in the middle of the room. My exit was distinctly less graceful.

Lyra was still laughing, when suddenly she hiccupped and vanished.

Like full-on disappeared from view. Just poof. "Lyra?" I called, slightly panicked. I glanced at Agnes and she stared back at me, wide-eyed.

"What in the salty whale's behind just happened?"

Another hiccup sounded and Lyra winked back into view. "Sorry about that," she hiccupped and vanished again. What on Earth?

"Where does she go when that happens?"

There was another hiccup and Lyra reappeared. "Whenever I sneeze or hiccup I tend to..." *Hiccup* And she was gone.

"I'm assuming the end of her sentence was that she vanishes," Agnes said dryly. "I don't think I've ever seen that before. What happens if she's driving?"

Hiccup This time, rather than trying to talk to us Lyra held her breath and just stared at us. Then she let out a gusty sigh. "Sorry. Bad habit. I was hoping that Garret Goul could fix it, but then he burned to a crisp, and I'm stuck dreading cold and flu season again."

"What was that?" I asked.

"A glitch," Lyra explained. "As Fae, we can have issues with our magic, but it only reflects back onto ourselves. I call mine my glitch. Whenever I hiccup or sneeze or fart with any type of force, I vanish."

"Where do you go?" Agnes asked, curiosity in her voice. She had leaned forward, craning her neck so that she looked like a goose preparing to strike.

Lyra shrugged her shoulders. "Sometimes to the countryside, once it was to Hawaii. Always nice places, but never a place I've been before."

"Have you ever gotten stuck somewhere?"

"Once my hiccups took me to Venice, then stopped. I spent a while trying to get them going again so I could get home."

"What happens if you're driving and you have to sneeze?"

"I don't drive."

"I have so many more questions," Agnes said as she drew in a deep breath. "Do people notice? Do you ever try to get out of things by inhaling pepper? Does the direction that you are facing when you hiccup affect which direction you go around the globe?"

"Yes, yes, and I hadn't thought about that, maybe."

"Do you..."

"Agnes," I said, cutting her off mid-question. It was a habit I knew she hated, but we were facing bigger problems. "Maybe, just maybe, right now, in the middle of a dead man's room, when we just found protection runes underneath his bed, isn't the time to be talking about this. I can help you make a list of questions that you can ask when we're out of here. I'll invite Lyra over for wine, and you can bombard her with questions if she's game."

Agnes growled—literally growled at me. "Don't treat me like a child. I know your mother is a whiny toddler, but I am not."

"I'll answer all of your questions," Lyra said. "I could use some friends who are just as weird as me. No offense."

"I turned you into a cat. There's no offense taken," I said with a smile. I didn't have many friends, and Lyra had a point that it would be a nice change of pace to have a friend who was an outcast like me.

"And you tell me to focus," Agnes snipped from behind me. "Hello, Pot, meet Kettle."

I rolled my eyes for only Lyra to see and turned back to Garret Goul's bed. The entire four-poster monstrosity seemed to loom larger in the dim light. The dark bedding made it seem way more ominous.

"Why would he need runes of protection?" I asked aloud.

"He was killed," Lyra said. "He probably knew it was coming and decided to try to get protection from it. But the question is, how did he know?"

"That rune is typically used for protection from other-worldly spirits," Agnes recited from memory. "It isn't used for physical beings. Think more along the lines of demons rather than humans."

It reminded me of the glow that Garret Goul's ring had made in the dark. The faint red light that I had convinced myself meant my eyes were tired. "Could he have needed protection from say, a demon-possessed item?"

Agnes's eyes snapped over to mine. "Possibly." She knew which direction my mind had gone.

So, apparently, did Lyra. "His ring," she said. "It was the only part of his body that wasn't burned. It was the only thing that survived the fire. It must mean that it was magical. Flesh burns at high heat and gold is a soft metal."

I nodded slowly. Demons were notorious for being fickle fiends and overreacting to things when upset. "But where had the demon come from? And why did it stay? Demons don't remain in one place because they want to. Something keeps them bound to this side of the void."

"Could he have had a bond with a demon?" Lyra asked, curiously.

Demon bonding was an epically bad idea. It came from dark magic and was better left untouched. It was the kind of magic that everyone whispers about behind their hands, yet no one knew how to access it and you can't just stumble across it. Like the Dark Web in the human world.

"So he summoned a demon and then died? That's suspicious." Lyra wrinkled her nose. "But why would it kill him? Especially if it was bound to him. Can they even do that?"

"And how crazy was he to summon a demon?" Agnes barked. "That kind of crazy is certifiable."

My head was spinning. If Garret Goul had summoned a demon, why would the demon have gone after Sabrina? Why go after someone who had nothing to do with your summoning? Unless Sabrina had been involved somehow? I shook my head.

"We can't speculate," I said to the room at large, but also to remind myself. Speculation didn't get us anywhere. "I have his journal and am working to decipher it. Maybe it will tell us more."

"Where did you get this journal from?" Lyra asked.

It took me a minute to remember that I hadn't been with her when I found the journal. So I quickly gave her the low-down on how it came into my possession.

"Good for you!" Lyra said. "Girl power to the max. Just don't let good-looking detective man realize that you are secretly a breaking-and-entering, journal-stealing badass. Men tend to get intimidated by that."

18

Moonlight Madness

DECIPHERING THE REST OF the journal took all afternoon and into the evening.

After Agnes and I returned to my room and shut the door, I picked up the journal and started coloring over the letters again. One hour had turned into two, which had turned into six, but the journal was finally coming together. I had gone through four golf pencils and copious amounts of coffee, which had the added effect of making me quite jittery. And it hadn't helped me stay on track. Some of the pages I had to do twice because my hands were shaking so much.

"Do you think that much caffeine is good for you?" Agnes asked. "Your blood pressure must be through the roof."

"I have to find out what this means. I have to get this done. In one day, the doors to this house will open, and the case will be turned over to the police."

"You mean the professionals who are trained to solve this? Just like I am not a coroner, you are not a detective. However, there is one right outside this room we could talk to. But no, we're stuck in this tiny room, with no discernible ventilation and you are covered in pencil shavings and lead."

"I want to be able to hand them something that helps," I muttered.

"Ok, we are diverging from sanity and traveling down the road to Cuckoo Town. There's hyperfocus and then there is obsession. The line is very thin, and you are so far over it, you wouldn't be able to see the line in your rearview mirror."

"Got to solve this."

Agnes rolled her eyes. "This is ridiculous." She disappeared.

I didn't have time to wonder where she had gone. Maybe she had gone to haunt the Dartmoths, or maybe she had gone to talk to Lyra since she had discovered another person who could hear her. It didn't matter. I ignored the raging hunger and the shaking limbs and continued.

Then, finally, I was done! I had the whole journal colored over and went back through and traced the remaining words with a pencil. I picked up the journal and began to read my handiwork.

April 2

The new ring has worked wonders. I shall have to thank Darcy for this idea. It's not every day that one finds a Demon ring. Especially with a demon that is so amenable to collaboration. Perhaps this could work.

April 7

Strangely, I don't need much sleep anymore. I can go for days at a time without sleep and not have my work suffer in the slightest. I am looking at inviting more groups of people to the manor. That way I can fully invest the time into helping them.

April 13

Strange things have been happening around the house. Things have been moved around. Small thing. Things most would not notice, but I do. I have asked the staff if they have moved the items. But each of them denies it. I swear that I had put a book back in the library but I just found it sitting on my bed. It is certainly strange. There must be something going on.

April 27

There's someone in my house. Someone bad. Or the house is watching me. Waiting for me to relax so that it can strike. I can't sleep. I want to, but when I close my eyes, I see things. Things that aren't right. I know in my gut that they are wrong, but I can't wake myself.

May 2

I put up the wards. Just like my Demon said. They will protect me from the evil in this house. Even the staff are turning against me. Darcy spoke to me with such an angry tone the other day. Darcy never speaks to me that way. He must be under the influence of the house. It must have gotten to him too.

May 15

Darcy informs me that a former client of mine has been writing me. Begging me to fix her again. Apparently, what I did in the past wasn't working now. I don't know why he would lie to me like that. Everything I have done has been perfect. Every spell was enacted perfectly. No one has been any the wiser. I don't know why he would tell me things that are not true. He keeps trying to paint it that my ring is making me crazy, but I know it's not. It is this house. It has always been against me. My ring is the only thing keeping me sane.

There was a knock on my door. I jolted, sharply, bumping my head on the wall behind the bed. I swore, rubbing the spot vigorously.

From beyond my door, I heard a chuckle, then a deep voice said, "Sounds like that hurt."

Silas.

I sprinted to the door and wrenched it open. His eyes widened slightly before a slow smile spread across his face. "You look like you've been working on the journal."

Self-consciencely my hand went to my hair. I had put it up some time ago into a messy bun and secured it with a pencil. I patted it, trying to tame the flyaways back into submission.

Silas grinned again. "It's kind of hot. Like a librarian fantasy."

"That's what you dream about? Librarians?"

Silas shrugged. "Reading is sexy." He leaned forward. "Are you going to invite me in?"

"What? Are you a vampire? Can't you just walk in yourself?"

Silas grinned widely. "My mom always taught me that it was bad manners to just enter a lady's quarters without her express permission."

"Your mother is right. Come on in." I stepped back, giving him space to walk inside. I shut the door behind me and turned back to see Silas surveying the room with a critical eye. The room looked like a tornado had passed through. The journal sat in the middle of the bed, surrounded by pencils, the cover torn open. Pencil shavings littered the once-pristine white sheets.

"I've been trying to get the journal done," I explained, "so that in a few days it can go with you to the police and they will have everything they need to make an arrest. Or at least figure out what's happening. I want to make things as easy as possible. I want to be helpful. Also, Garret Goul was going crazy. Something happened and I think it's tied to that ring that he wore. It was demon-possessed. He said that the demon was friendly and ready to work together with him, but I'm not so sure. Maybe..."

"Whoa, whoa, whoa. Slow down!" Silas held up his hands, palms facing me. "I can see why Agnes came and got me." He let out a low chuckle.

"Evidently she wants you to have a partner to solve things with, or someone to pull you away."

"Agnes came and got you?" I asked, dumbfounded. "How do you know it was her?"

"I don't really. Just suddenly all the things that were in my suitcase began taking themselves out of my suitcase, one at a time." He chuckled "She made all my boxers do a dance. I don't know whether to be offended that she keeps touching my stuff or to find it all funny."

"With Agnes, it's hard to tell. The default setting is to just let her do her thing. Otherwise, she gets fussy. She's like a grumpy toddler."

"I took it as a sign that I should probably come check on you," he said.

"You took Agnes playing with your boxers as a sign to come check on me?" I repeated.

"Well, when she started making one pair dance down the hallway toward your door, yes." He sat down in the middle of the bed. "Why don't you tell me what you've found—a little slower this time."

And so I did. Reading him excerpts from the journal as I went.

When I finished, Silas looked pensive. "So he was losing it? Over the demon ring?"

"I think the ring was possessing him. It was making him paranoid."

Silas ran a hand through his hair. "That doesn't explain what killed him. Unless we think it was the demon itself. But there's no way that we can even check that. Demons don't admit to things on a good day."

"Maybe there's more in the journal that we're missing. Maybe we can head back to his study and see if there is something we missed there." I glanced at the clock on the nightstand. "It's only nine-thirty. We could still go and check it out. "

Silas shifted his weight from foot to foot, suddenly looking a little awkward. "I can't." Then his voice dropped almost to a whisper. "It's the full moon tonight."

I froze.

I had never been around a werewolf during a shift. What had come down through the pipeline was that werewolves' transformations were unpredictable. Especially when the full moon was shining through the trees. They tended to bite and not in the love-bite or sexy I'm-going-to-bang-you way. More like in the rip-your-arm-off-and-feed-it-to-you way. "Umm...is...do you need me to go?"

Silas's mouth quirked up. "This is your room."

"Okay, so, do you need to go? Or do you need help moving a heavy object in front of the door?"

"What do you think happens during a werewolf shift exactly?" Silas looked amused, as though arm ripping off was funny.

"You get moon-possessed and a large wolf comes out. And unlike a lot of white women, I have a sense of self-preservation and know not to approach a wild animal, no matter how cute they are. Otherwise, I would 100% try to pet a lynx, but they are big angry kitties, and again, self-preservation."

"That's not exactly what happens," Silas smiled. "Yes, we get moon-possessed, but as long as you don't run and we aren't hungry, we're usually pretty tame. Shifting is a lot of work. The drive to chase and destroy would take too much effort on top of that."

"I'm assuming of course that you aren't hungry right now?"

Silas laughed softly. "I ate before I came over. And I won't take a bite out of you unless you want me to. And even then it wouldn't be a bite that you wouldn't want."

"He means a sexy bite," Agnes hissed, appearing from thin air beside me. "And I'm going to go again because I think things are just about to get interesting."

"My wolf is...unique," Silas continued, oblivious to Agnes passing in and out of the room like she was sushi on a conveyor belt. "Most wolves age as their human ages. Mine, well, it's the reason I'm here." He looked a little put out. Like he was embarrassed by what he was about to say.

"Why?" I asked, genuinely curious. He clearly could shift, so what was the issue exactly?

"My wolf never aged," Silas explained. At my befuddled look, he continued, "he stayed a puppy. He didn't get older. He has always been and will always be a pup."

"A puppy?" I asked. I was slightly ashamed to admit that my voice did that raising thing at the end of the sentence. It sounded like I was hopeful that he was going to be my puppy.

"Yeah. I don't run as fast as the other wolves, and it's something my packmates poke fun at. I'm an eternal puppy."

"Just to be clear," I said, "you are of age, right? Even if your wolf isn't."

Silas's lips quirked again. I was getting used to his half-smiles, and I rather liked them. They felt special and just for me. Again, crazy, we were in a closed environment with two dead bodies (ok, one was actually a pile of ash), a married couple, and Lyra, who, though she thought Silas was hot, wasn't interested. It wasn't like I had a lot of competition for his attention.

"I was kind of hoping," Silas said, "that I could stay here during my shift. My wolf likes being around people. It soothes him. I promise it's not as scary as it seems in movies."

"You don't howl at the full moon?"

"Only when I want to, but I promise I am in complete control when it happens. I just," he paused. "I just trust you."

My insides warmed, and Silas trusted me. He came to me for his shift.

"Sure," I heard myself say, "you can stay here with me during your shift."

19

Wolfy Tales and Demon Wiles

"THIS IS NOT EXACTLY what I had in mind when I went to get him," Agnes grumbled, as we sat on the floor an hour later, holding a squirming wolf pup in my arms.

Silas's wolf may have been little, but he sure was strong. He was about 20 pounds of pure muscle, with teeth like little needles. And I don't know what he was talking about, but he certainly wasn't in full control of his wolf.

Not that the wolf pup had done anything to hurt me, but, man, was he rowdy. It was like trying to wrangle a fluffy cow with teeth.

The first thing he did was to attempt to pull the blanket off the bed with his teeth. He ripped the corner off.

Then he went for the leg of the wardrobe and started gnawing through it with the determination of a beaver, sending little wooden splinters all over the room. When I chased him, he took off like a Tasmanian devil, racing under the bed, over the bed, and around the nightstand, before I finally caught him.

He reminded me about why, if I ever did get a dog, it would most likely be an older, wiser, and less neurotic one. The neurotic didn't bother me—hello! I had Agnes as a familiar—but the out-of-control puppy crazy sure did.

I wrapped my arms around the squirming puppy. "Settle," I commanded, using my firmest voice.

The wolf pup yipped at me and tried to lick my face, but he missed and got my hair instead, which he promptly choked on and tried to spit out.

"Do you think this is what he's like in real life? Outside of the manor?" Agnes asked. I shot her a dry look. "What?" she said defensively. "It's a valid question. What if he chases people around and licks them?"

"He's a police officer."

"He claims he's a police officer. What if he's actually a stripper with a special licking kink?"

"Somehow I doubt that," I said as wolf Silas wriggled free again and raced around the room once more, launching himself headfirst into my suitcase. I sighed, loudly. Is this what people with toddlers have to deal with? Having them get into literally everything?

"Back beast!" Agnes shouted. "Don't grab her underwear, you horn dog!" She chuckled. "Get it? A wolf's a dog."

"You know the joke is less funny when you explain it," I said, dryly.

"You're just bitter that he's more interested in your panties when he's in wolf form than when he's human."

"You don't know me," I mumbled under my breath, but of course, Agnes heard, if her snort of derision was anything to go by. "What do we do while Kujo is tearing apart the room?" I asked.

"Well, it's not like we can put on a movie," she said. "Maybe we keep reading his journal and seeing what shakes loose from that?"

"The ring!"

Agnes shot me a bland look. "Your mind jumps to odd and mysterious places. Elaborate and tell me how you got there."

"I have the ring. The ring that Garret Goul mentioned in his journal. The ring that I think was possessing him. We could look at it."

"Look at it how?"

"I don't know. See if the demon wants to talk?"

"Let me see get this straight. You're going to take a demon-possessed ring out, look at it, and try to communicate with the crazy-inducing demon inside? The same demon that drove a grown man to lose his marbles?"

"Yes."

"The demon that might have the power to manipulate other people's minds and get them to believe that they are cured, when in fact they are not?"

"Yes."

"Do you hear how stupid that sounds? Like, the kind of stupid that makes the wolf puppy, currently chewing a hole through your thongs, seem smart?"

I looked over and saw that Silas was indeed chewing the string of one of my thongs. I wrestled it away from him. "Bad dog."

Agnes rolled her eyes. "You've got to be kidding me."

"So you don't think it's a good idea?"

"No! I think it's perhaps the worst idea you've had since we arrived. And since that time, you've done magic. Poor choice! Decided to venture into a dark tunnel alone. Poor choice! Then investigated the room of a dead man."

"I had Lyra with me on that one."

"Not my point."

"What else is there to do?"

"Literally anything else! How have you survived to be 28? How have you not been eaten by an alligator or something?"

"It's the Pacific Northwest," I reminded her with a shrug. "We don't have alligators."

Agnes glared at me. "I can tell you are being purposely obtuse, and I assumed it's because you don't want to admit that I'm right. I've known you for nearly a decade. I know you're not usually this stupid."

"I want to solve this."

"Why?"

"I want to be good at something."

"Take up tennis or that new sport, pickleball. Hunting down killers, isn't it!"

"Maybe it is," I argued.

"My god," Agnes flopped down on the floor. Right on top of the puppy. Since she was a ghost she didn't squish him, but he let out a loud yelp and raced backward. Running into a ghost is like getting doused in ice water. "Fine. But I am not going to be the one pulling you from his clutches. If you get possessed by a demon, I'm out. I would choose to hang out with your mother."

And that's how you know that an idea is a terrible one. Agnes hated my mother.

"I want to be good at something that is slightly outside of my wheelhouse."

"The moon is slightly outside of your wheelhouse. But somehow, it's still closer than being a detective. And wanting to be good at something is no reason to provoke—what is sure to be—a pissed-off demon."

I rolled my eyes. "I think it'll be fine. I've got you and Silas here to defend me!"

Agnes cast a dubious glance down at puppy Silas who had discovered that he had a tail and was chasing it. "Yes. He seems on top of it at the moment." She rolled her eyes so hard I was amazed that they didn't disappear into her head.

"What's the harm?" I insisted. "I put on the ring and just see. If it works, then maybe I can figure out who killed Garret Goul. If it doesn't, then it doesn't."

"And if the demon sucks your soul in through the ring and devours it whole?"

"That can't happen."

"You don't know that! You've never dealt with a demon."

"Neither have you! What's the worst that can happen?"

Agnes shot me a look. "We've discussed the soul-sucking, right?"

I shook my head at her, then pulled the ring out of my pocket and looked at it. The golden band sat heavy in my hand, looking plain and boring, except of course for the gawdy-looking eagle. Was it weighed down by the weight of an inhabitant, perhaps? "I think it's fine. It looks harmless."

Tentatively I slid the ring on my finger. I looked over to see Agnes cowering, her hands over her head, her knees bent as though she were bracing herself for impact. "It's a ring, not a bomb, Agnes."

"You sure?"

"And it's not like it's going to hit you either. You're already dead!"

"I have no desire to have my soul sucked into a black hole of demoness, thank you very much."

"Nothing's happened," I glanced at the ring. Nothing glowed, nothing changed about the surface of the ring. I hung my head. To be honest I was slightly disappointed. Agnes had a point about it being reckless, but I had genuinely wanted to solve this, to be useful.

I didn't love being my mother's assistant. It wasn't a dream career, but trying to figure out what happened to Garret Goul? That was fun and exciting! Something that was sorely lacking in my life.

"You know, if it's excitement you crave, I could help you."

"That's nice, Agnes, but I don't like your version of excitement."

"What?" Agnes snapped. "That's rude, why would you even say that to me."

"You wanted to give me excitement."

"No, I don't."

"You just said you did."

"I didn't say anything, you fool. What are you blathering on about?"

"Yes, you did. I heard you tell me about excitement."

"No."

"Yes."

Agnes stopped dead in her tracks, staring at me like I had grown an extra head.

"Good one." Only Agnes's mouth didn't move with the words. Neither did mine. And since Silas was still in his wolf pup form, he didn't say it either.

"Poppy…" Agnes said slowly, taking a hesitant step away from me. "Did you hear a voice that wasn't mine?"

"Well, it depends," the voice said, only, once again, Agnes's mouth didn't move. Nothing moved.

"Crap," I said aloud.

"Swearing is very unbecoming," the voice said again, a distasteful tone saturating it.

"Agnes," I said. "There's someone in my head. You don't hear them?"

"She doesn't," the voice said.

At the same time, Agnes went "No."

"Crap," I muttered again.

"So uncouth," the voice muttered. "What has this generation come to?"

"Who are you?" I asked. Trying to keep the panic out of my voice. This was going downhill faster than a toboggan on ice.

"I don't like this," Agnes said. "Take the ring off."

"The bitter old biddy is no fun, is she? I could have her gone in a heartbeat if you wanted me to. It must be terrible with a person like that residing in your head." The voice sighed gustily. "It must be so hard never being normal. I could fix it for you."

"Who are you?" I repeated, trying to inject steel into my voice.

"Don't you know?" The voice wheedled in my head. "I'm a better you."

20

"A Better Me" Still Couldn't Have Lactose

"A BETTER ME?" I asked, dumbfounded. "That's a stupid name."

"Don't be obtuse," the voice snapped. "If you want a name, it's Darwin."

"Darwin the demon? Not very original," I muttered.

Agnes scoffed from across the room. "Darwin? That's the best he's got?"

"The two of you are quite rude." Darwin's voice was distasteful. "Witches, who think they know everything. It's pathetic."

"Now, there's no need to be rude, Darwin," I said. It was bad form to mock a Demon, but it wasn't as if he was a paragon of good virtue either.

"Stating a fact is not rude. Now, where was I?"

"You were telling me that you could give me everything I've ever wanted. Tell me, does that include love?"

"Of course as much love as you'd like."

"Money?"

"Naturally."

"Magic that works?"

"I'm saddened that you even have to ask."

"Freedom from my lactose intolerance?"

There was a pregnant pause. "What?"

"I'd like to not have issues with dairy, please. I'd like to eat ice cream."

The pause went on longer this time. I waited. Finally, "You are mocking me," Darwin said.

"Not mocking, but I highly doubt you do all this for free."

Darwin was quiet again. "I do not. But as my last master can attest, I am very good at what I do."

"Your last master is dead."

"Dead or alive—it has no bearing on me. I served that master dutifully."

"He was burned to a crisp. Did you have anything to do with that, Darwin?"

"Of course, I did not. I'm offended you'd even ask. I don't kill people. Never have in my entire existence."

"But do you know who did kill them?"

"You'd need to be more specific. Franz Ferdinand? The Tsar of Russia? I know a lot of things."

"Garret Goul and Sabrina Cross."

"I know who killed the girl. I would assume the former is one and the same."

"It seems weird to me that you aren't more torn up about your master's death."

"Wahhh..." Darwin let out a long and sarcastic-sounding cry. "I don't care what happens in the human realm. It has no bearing on me."

That seemed cold and unfeeling to me. I felt like he should care at least a little bit. What if the person who was wearing his ring was a serial killer?

"I don't care if they are," Darwin muttered, startling me. I forgot that he could hear my thoughts as well as my words. I wondered if that was what Garret Goul had been going through. Hearing Darwin all the time.

"Garret Goul had many problems. The least of which was me being in his head."

"What kind of problems?" I said aloud, wanting Agnes to be able to hear also.

"Everyone wants to be rich and famous. Everyone wants to make an impact. But everyone also wants to cut corners to get there. They will step on other people and crush them into the ground to make their point. Garret Goul was no exception."

"What did he do to get his own way?" I asked.

"All kinds of nasty things. Cheating, lying, hurting, killing. Whatever it took, he did. That's what made him such a perfect host. I tend to like those who are a bit morally gray, for obvious reasons."

"I've heard nothing but good things about Garret Goul," I insisted. "His program was life-changing."

"My program was life-changing, you mean? I was the brains behind the operation. It was me all along. He did so little he was practically obsolete."

"Kind of a harsh way to talk about him."

"Not harsh, if it's true."

"Tell me more about him," I insisted. "And tell me more about who killed Sabrina."

"I can't tell you who killed her. Only that they had a very specific reason for wanting her dead. Kind of a niche reason, if you ask me."

"Was it you, Darwin?"

"Of course not! Again, I don't kill. I'm insulted you would even ask me that—twice! No, the person who killed her, knew her before she came here."

"That tells me nothing," I said, frustrated beyond measure.

"Well, think about it! Put your brain to work. Someone who knows death well is a harbinger of death. Who here might have had a motive to kill her? Someone who has probably killed before?"

"The Dartmoths!" I nearly shouted. "If it wasn't you, Darwin, it had to have been them!"

"Who are you talking to?" The deep voice came from behind me. I spun around. Silas stood before me, looking slightly weary. He was shirtless and his chest was a perfect bronze color.

I gawked. "What?"

"I said, who are you talking to?" Silas asked again, frowning.

"Darwin," I said. I shook my head, trying to clear it. I had seen good-looking men before. Admittedly not many, but some. I slid the ring off my finger. "Darwin is the demon who lives inside Garret Goul's ring. He said that whoever killed Garret and Sabrina had to be someone who knows death. Someone who has killed before."

"You were possessed by the ring?"

"No! Darwin just spoke to me after I put the ring on. He swears that he didn't do it, but he won't tell me the name. He's only giving me clues."

"He's speaking to you? How long has he been speaking to you?"

"Just since I put the ring on a few minutes ago." I glanced over at the clock and saw that it was nearing five in the morning. "I guess it's been a few hours now. Time just flew by." I wondered vaguely if Darwin had something to do with the time slipping by. "But he said that the person or persons who killed Garret and Sabrina knew how to kill. It has to be Sean and Delilah. That's why they were trying to distract us from what was happening. They knew all along that they were the ones behind it."

I deflated slightly. "But we have no proof other than Darwin."

"I think I've heard enough," Silas interrupted, his usually jovial tone was grim. "I think we need to go confront the killer."

21
Clue Just Got Personal

IT WAS LIKE A game of Clue. All the characters assembled in the library, standing stoically, nervous expressions on every face. Well, except Agnes, who was practically bouncing up and down on the balls of her feet and salivating.

"I wonder who it is!" She said, her tone gleeful. "I bet it's Delilah Dartmoth. What other reason does she have for being here? She paid her way in to keep an eye on her husband. If that tells you anything, it's that she doesn't trust him."

I too suspected the Dartmoths. Sean insisted that he had an alibi for Sabrina's death in that he didn't drink blood. But the fact remained that they knew that Garret Goul was a fraud before his death. They both knew about Sabrina's issues. Maybe they thought she had heard Garret Goul's final moments and could pin it on them. It wasn't so far-fetched to assume that they would have killed to keep Sean's secret.

Then there was Lyra, the Fae who didn't quite fit in with the rest of us. As far as I knew she vanished to exotic places when she sneezed. It wasn't as big a problem as the rest of us and wouldn't require fixing from the magical master. So why had she been invited?

"Thank you everyone for joining me here," Silas started, speaking like he was at the reading of the world's most boring will. "I know that it's been a stressful few days here, and this hasn't been the experience any of us expected at all."

Agnes stomped her foot. "Get to the good stuff, Detective Hottie! This is as boring as watching paint dry."

"After careful consideration of all the facts, I have come to some conclusions." Silas began pacing around the room. "We know that the murder of Garret Goul probably had something to do with the fact that he was a fraud. We also know that whoever killed Garret Goul probably killed Sabrina to keep her from speaking out. We also know that both Sabrina and Garret Goul were killed in two different, but anger-fueled manners. Garret Goul was presumably lit on fire, burning to death and Sabrina was killed by blunt force trauma to the head, causing massive bleeding. Both deaths point to homicide, and considering the lack of clues around the body, it leads me to believe that the culprit was being controlled by some external magic."

"Demon magic," Agnes sang. "Someone is possessed by a demon."

"I think we need to understand that these murders were not done by a person who had control over what was happening. Indeed, there is no reason for me to believe that they were premeditated. I think they were spur-of-the-moment actions brought on by great stress."

"He's so smart," Agnes cooed, "making it seem like the person made a mistake. A classic move for a seasoned detective. It draws out the suspects and makes them put their guard down. You really should date him when we get out of here."

"I take no pleasure in doing this," Silas said as he came to stand beside me, facing everyone else. "But I'm afraid it has to be done."

Without warning, Silas turned to me, pity in his eyes. "Poppy Seymour, you're under arrest for the murders of Sabrina Cross and Garret Goul. You will be detained in a secure location until the doors open today at noon, at which point you will be taken into custody. You have the right to remain..."

"What?" Agnes's shout could have rattled the paint off the walls. Silas slowly and carefully slid the cuffs in his hand around my wrists, clicking them into place.

It was as though the cool metal unleashed some fight or flight in me. As though I woke up and chose violence. I began thrashing against his hold, straining my wrists. "What? Are you kidding me? I didn't do this! I didn't do anything. Why are you arresting me?" I thrashed harder against Silas's hold. "I didn't kill anyone." My voice was fast becoming a sob.

Though Silas's hold was firm, his voice was gentle. "Poppy," he said soothingly, "I don't think you did it on purpose. But I saw you while you were possessed by the demon ring that you had. I saw it's hold on you. You were possessed. You weren't in control. You didn't even notice me."

I glanced wildly around the room. Waiting for someone to clue me in on the joke. Lyra's face was etched with sympathy. Delilah Dartmoth looked smug and Sean Dartmoth was avoiding my gaze. Darcy looked shocked. "It wasn't me!" I shouted, my voice ringing so loudly off the walls that it almost made my ears hurt. Everyone winced. "That was the only time I was in communication with Darwin. I wasn't possessed."

"And I firmly believe that you believe that," Silas said. "But your magic is uncontrollable. Chaos magic often is. If you let it slip, even a little bit, you risk hurting others." His voice dropped low again "I don't think you meant to hurt anyone, Poppy. I will do my best to keep you safe and explain the situation to my superiors. I think they will also find that your actions were not your own. Nothing you did was intentional. Please," he said dropping his voice even lower.

I felt tears escaping my eyes and tracking down my cheeks. "I thought you said that my Chaos magic was special. I never would have told you about any of it if I had known that it would be used against me. I didn't do this. I'd never kill anyone. That isn't me! Even when my magic is pure chaos."

"I'm sorry," Silas whispered, his voice cracking. "I am so sorry." He pulled gently on my arm in an attempt to get me to move.

I resisted. "No."

"I don't think she did it." Lyra chimed in from the doorway.

"Thinking isn't knowing, Fae," Delilah snapped. "The detective has evidence, otherwise—with his speech the other day—he wouldn't be arresting her."

"I'm going to ram her pointy teeth into her upper jaw," Agnes growled. "Then I'm going to cut the formerly sexy detective's fluffy tail off and feed it to the vegetable vampire. The rat bastard."

The lights above us began to shake.

Silas glanced up at the ceiling and then back down again. "Agnes," he whispered. "You're not helping her case."

The lights stopped shaking abruptly.

"Is Agnes her alter ego? Does this go deeper than we thought?" Delilah asked snidely.

"No," Agnes shouted, her whole body vibrating with fury. "But I am the one who will haunt you until the cows come home. You think shaking lights are a big deal. Let's see who's laughing after I start moving stuff around in your house. I bet it's nice and organized too. Well, not for long."

I didn't respond. To Delilah or Agnes. My heart physically hurt. I had trusted Silas. I had told him about Agnes. Agnes wasn't something I shared with most people, mostly because it got thrown back in my face time and time again. And yet here it was—same story, different day. My stomach churned uncomfortably.

"I'm going to put you in your room now," Silas said. "Please, please don't resist. It'll make it so much harder."

"Give up the puppy love," Delilah snapped. "She's a murderer. She deserves to be locked up, not your words of sympathy."

"Will you shut it?" Lyra barked, so loudly that it made my ears ring. "She might be an accidental murderer—and even that I doubt. But you are a thousand times worse. At least if she killed someone, it wasn't intentional. But you, you're just mean. And that's something that can't be fixed. So shut up and leave her alone. Go back to your coffin!"

Delilah huffed loudly, tossing her blonde hair over her shoulder, and flounced out of the room.

"Didn't think she had it in her," Agnes sounded impressed. "I might just accept her into the fold yet. Detective Stupid-Face, however, is another story. I plan on haunting him, and not in the way I originally intended to."

"Silas," I whispered. Silas's eyes snapped to me, his handsome face was etched in remorse. "Please don't do this. It wasn't me. You know it wasn't me."

He shook his head. "I have to go where the evidence points me."

"What about the protection symbols under Garret Goul's bed? What about the fact that he was a fraud?"

Silas sighed heavily. "Look Poppy, you have to understand that all those pieces of evidence were brought to my attention by you."

He was right. I found the symbols under Garret Gouls' bed. I was the one who determined that Garret Goul's journal revealed his descent into madness. I had brought up the demon. It had all been me.

"It won't be that bad," Silas insisted. "You'll have to stay in your room for the rest of the morning, but as soon as the doors unlock at noon, we can go out into the real world and figure this out. It'll be much easier when we haven't been trapped in this house for days on end. It'll provide some clarity." He pulled me gently along, leaving Lyra standing alone in the room with Darcy. My last glimpse was of the door to the library slamming closed.

We walked in near silence to the bedrooms, the only sound the slapping of our footsteps on the hardwood floor. I made sure that I stomped. Outside my door, Silas stopped and gently took off the handcuffs.

I looked at him, confused.

"I'm going to lock the door," Silas said, "I'll also be right outside this door so you don't need to wear handcuffs in your room."

"My cell, you mean?" I snapped at him.

"I'm just happy to know that there's not another way out of your room. I wouldn't want you searching around the house for clues or answers when you should be staying in detention."

I frowned at him. He knew good and well about the tunnel that ran from my room to the library. But, Silas didn't so much as blink as the lie rolled off his lips. That's when I realized that he was giving me a chance. A chance to do more digging, a chance to clear my name and discover the real killer.

I wasn't about to sit idly by and let that opportunity pass.

22

Cinderella and Carrots

THERE WAS A MURDERER out there. A murderer who knew— as I knew—that it wasn't me. And I had no doubt they would take me out if they could. They would be looking for any and all opportunities to make sure I was silenced for good.

"Cinderella, Cinderella! Night and day, I'm Cinderella," Agnes sang at the top of her lungs. Her gray hair had escaped her French twist to fall across the back of her neck. "Move the wardrobe! Chase the werewolf! Solve a murder, Cinderella."

"Agnes," I warned, my voice tired. Agnes wasn't a great singer, and right now her high-pitched singing was grating on my nerves as she moved the wardrobe out of the way to expose the tunnel behind.

"Sheesh, you sure are ornery," Agnes snorted. "I guess I'll give you a pass since you were just in handcuffs, but I'm trying to make light of the situation. Don't get your panties in a bunch."

"I'm sorry," I muttered. "I didn't mean to snap at you." In reality, I was tired, my body was aching from numerous nights of not sleeping well. And that included the all-nighter last night while I was communicating with Darwin. And I was pissed at Silas.

As I debated what my next move was going to be, someone dropped off breakfast for me, opening the door, and sliding the food inside like I was a common prisoner. My only hope was that it wasn't from the same storage fridge where they were keeping the body of Sabrina. Agnes wouldn't go check.

I needed to strategize. You're only as good as your best-laid plans. And I wasn't going to go down without a fight. And I sure as shit wasn't going to sit idly by and wait for the police to solve the crime. Silas had botched it on his own, even if he was trying to make it up to me in his own way.

I walked to the entrance of the tunnel, staring at the gaping hole in the wall that led down into blackness. I raised my arm and waved it. The torches snapped on as though they had been called.

"Before we go, run through the plan with me one more time," Agnes whispered. "We head down the tunnel, up into Garret Goul's office. Then our objective is to go down the hall and down the stairs to the butler's quarters."

"Exactly. Without being seen, which means that I'm going to need you as a lookout."

"What would you do if your familiar were a cat? Or God forbid, a toad?"

"I'd be going to prison," I muttered.

"When you get out of here," Agnes smirked. "I expect to be gifted the shirtless firefighter's calendar. Especially since I won't be seeing the sexy—yet stupid—detective shirtless. You owe me some shirtless men."

"I can do that."

"But seriously," Agnes continued, "why the butler? Do you think he did it?"

"I don't know," I ran my fingers through my hair in agitation. "But he's the one who knew Garret Goul the best. He was also here when Sabrina came through the first time. He must know more than he's letting on." He has to be able to help. But I didn't say that last part out loud.

"I can't go to Silas," I stated. "We know that's a bad idea. Lyra could still be a suspect, but she doesn't know any more than I do. And the Dartmoths hate me and think I'm a murderer. That leaves Darcy. He's the only one who could help."

"And if he takes one look at you and attacks because you killed his friend and boss?"

I swallowed thickly. "I guess that's a chance I'm just going to have to take. What choice do I have?"

"None," Agnes nodded. "Let's do this!"

And we headed down into the tunnel.

I was exceedingly grateful that—unlike the rest of the house—the tunnel was a straight shot. I didn't have to worry about getting lost or falling through a door that led to nowhere. It was a one-stop shop.

As I hurried along the tunnel, the flames from the torches seemed to usher me forward, the light prompting me to break into a jog.

"Do not expend all your energy on the tunnel part," Agnes said, huffing behind me. "You don't eat all the chips and guacamole before your order even arrives. Besides, we don't run, unless something is chasing us. So save your energy for when something is chasing us."

"Agnes, we have to move quickly. The doors unseal at noon." When we left the room, it had been close to eleven. There wasn't a lot of time left before the doors opened and I would be handed over to the police. I should have started earlier, I should have left right away but instead, I had wasted time. That was stupid.

The tunnel evened out, drawing up toward the wooden panel that I knew was the secret entrance to Garret Goul's office. I pushed the hidden button, and the lever slid the door open.

"You should have let me check if there was anyone in the room before you did that," Agnes hissed at me. "For all your 'hurry up and go' attitude you shouldn't be taking chances."

I peeked my head through the opening into the study. It was blessedly empty. "The coast is clear." I wiggled out and made my way over toward the double doors, skirting the desk.

With each creak of the floorboards under my feet, I felt sure that doors were going to swing open and reveal someone who would turn me over to Silas again. And at that point, it would be game over.

"Agnes, can you check the hallway for me?"

"On it," Agnes replied, keeping her voice low, even though no one could hear her but me and Lyra. Then she vanished.

I waited, studying my shoes. The seconds ticked by slowly. Each breath that I took felt like an eternity.

Then Agnes was back. "This hallway is clear. I don't know about the next one. I swear I could feel you breathing down the back of my neck."

I swallowed and yanked the door open, revealing the dimly lit hallway beyond. Though it was nearly noon, the only light came through the stained-glass window at the end. I crept forward, trying to keep my footsteps light, but each step sounded like a herd of elephants.

"Holy cow, could you breathe any louder?" Agnes hissed at me. "It's like a bear in hibernation."

"Shh," I whispered.

"You, shh," Agnes whispered back. "I don't like when you tell me what to do."

We crept down the hallway, heading toward the stairs that would lead to the main entrance. From there we would need to take the stairs down to Darcy's room in the basement.

As we made our way toward the front entrance, I realized that I wasn't alone.

"Take the bags and put them right by the doorway, dear," Delilah was saying in her nasally voice. "I want to be ready to go the instant that those doors open. I have hated every minute of our time here, and I can't wait to get back home."

"Yes, dear," Sean said.

The rustle of bags, and the dull thud that they made when they were set down echoed through the hallway. I was stuck. Delilah and Sean were waiting right by the door. I shot a panicked glance at Agnes but didn't dare make a sound. With their vampire hearing, I couldn't risk it. I was surprised that they hadn't heard me with my heavy breathing and pounding heart.

Agnes blinked. "I'm on it, one diversion of vampire proportions coming right up." And with that, she vanished.

I stayed frozen where I was at. Not daring to move a muscle.

"Only 45 minutes until we're out of this hell hole," Delilah complained loudly. "And luckily she'll be in police custody. Hopefully, they won't make us stay for a statement. I feel as though I have been traumatized enough."

"Yes, dear," Sean said. If I hadn't heard him speak in complete sentences during his confession,

I would have wondered if he only ever agreed with her.

"Once we get out, I plan on taking a nice long bubble bath and hiding away from everyone for a long time. Though we probably should donate to Serenity Seymour's campaign. Show her that—even if her daughter is a killer—we still believe in her ability to lead our town."

"Yes..." Sean trailed off suddenly.

"What is it?" Delilah asked, her tone sharp. "What's wrong?"

"Nothing," Sean sounded unsure. "It's nothing...just..."

"Just, what?"

"I thought I saw a carrot."

"What?" Delilah asked.

"I thought I saw a carrot, dangling in midair, just down the hallway toward the kitchen." Sean was clearly confused.

"Oh dear," Delilah fretted, her tone more soothing and gentler than I had ever imagined. "Is your blood sugar low again? I knew we should have gotten something for you to eat at breakfast time. Dead body in the fridge be damned. Come on," she said and I heard the distinct sound of footsteps. "We've got to find you something to eat before you pass out."

With that, the Darthmoths took off toward the kitchen, which was mercifully in the other direction, away from Darcy's room.

As soon as they were gone, Agnes popped back into existence beside me.

"Agnes," I breathed. "You are a goddess among ghosts."

Agnes preened. "You think so?"

"A pure genius."

"Stop it, you're making me blush," she fanned herself. "I almost chose a tomato but I thought a nice juicy carrot would be better."

"It worked perfectly," I said, cracking a smile at her.

I turned and hurried down the stairs, Agnes hot on my heels. I leaped over the bags lying in the middle of the floor and then raced down the final set of stairs to Darcy's room.

The hallway below was dark, no light came in from any windows. The bulb in the middle of the hallway was close to burning out, its dim light flickering on and off.

Darcy's room was at the end of the hallway, the wooden door plain and boring, completely at odds with the rest of the house. "Here goes nothing," I said. I raised my fist and knocked.

The door swung open, revealing darkness beyond. It was as quiet as the grave.

23

Cobwebs, Runes and One Suspicious Tortoise

I FUMBLED AROUND UNTIL I felt a light switch and flicked it on. The room was bathed in a pale glow. Darcy was nowhere to be seen.

"Thank goodness," Agnes breathed, "I was convinced that we were going to find another dead body. I don't think I can take anymore."

"Yeah, Delilah would have convinced even me after that," I muttered, stepping into the space.

Darcy's room was neat and impersonal. There weren't any pictures or personal effects. The bed was made with military precision, the pillows straightened to perfection. "What do we do now?" I asked aloud to the quiet room.

"We could wait for him," Agnes suggested. "We might give him a heart attack, but I don't know if wandering around the hallways is the best idea."

I sighed and took a seat on the neatly made bed. Was it weird to walk into someone's room and just sit on their bed? Probably. But I was past the point of caring. I just hoped that the sheets were clean.

I glanced around. There was one singular book on the floor next to the bed that looked like Darcy had been reading. *Demons and Their Masters*.

I frowned and bent down to retrieve the book. The spine was cracked and worn, as if it had been opened and read numerous times. The book fell open to a dog-eared page about demon possession through objects. A faint chill went up my spine.

I set the book back on the floor. I had had enough of demon-possessed items. As I laid the book back down, I noticed something else. A small pile of wood shavings scattered across the carpet, underneath the bed.

Curiosity got the better of me. I slid off the bed and knelt beside it, peering underneath. In the corner of the bed was a fresh carving etched into the wooden bed frame. A small symbol, like a trident with three straight lines that pointed directly up into the air. The Rune of Protection, Algiz. I stood up again.

The chills that had erupted along my skin turned into full-blown shivers.

"Agnes," I said, as calmly as I could, "we need to get out of here. Right now."

"What?"

"I'm afraid that won't be happening," said a deep voice from behind me. I whipped around and saw Darcy standing in the doorway, twisting his hands in agitation.

"You just couldn't let it go, could you?" he barked. His voice was sharp, not the quiet, gentle tone he'd used before. He stretched his fingers out before him and I saw the thin white band of skin that ringed the middle finger on his right hand. A distinct mark, lighter than the rest of his hand. One that I recognized easily. Realization hit like a freight train.

"You're not Darcy. You're Garret Goul, aren't you?"

A twisted smile turned up the corners of Garret Goul's mouth. It was a smile that made him look like the Joker in Batman. "What gave it away?"

"What *did* give it away?" Agnes asked. "I mean, I knew it was the butler who always did it, but the butler that's actually the master?"

"You have a white line on your finger," I stated. "The ring was sitting there, but now it's gone. It's on the wrong hand and finger to be a wedding ring, so it had to have been the ring that Garret Goul always wore. You twist it when you're nervous, but, without the ring, it just looks like you're wringing your hands."

"What's more, the symbols under Darcy's bed are the same ones that were carved under Garret Goul's bed. Only these are fresh—like they have been done in the last few days. You obviously moved from your room to his."

Another thought occurred to me, hitting like lightning. "You also were never around Sabrina at the same time as the rest of us. It's because you knew she would recognize you and address you as Garret Goul and your cover would be blown. So you made sure she was in her room when the first body was found." I stared at him, as level as I could, even though I wanted to scream and run.

"You killed the real Darcy because he was going to turn you in. He knew you'd lost control and you were lying to people. He figured it out when he got Sabrina's emails. Then when Sabrina turned up, you had to kill her too, before she could out you as a fraud."

Garret Goul stared at me directly, the corner of his eye twitching. "You know, I thought you were kind of stupid. I mean you landed yourself in the middle of everything. It was so easy to feed that frivolous Delilah Dartmoth words and have her repeat them back to frame you.

"But you did figure it out, didn't you? Better than the detective. He really must be incompetent if he let you escape."

I neglected to tell him that Silas probably knew good and well that I had escaped.

"What a sick and twisted little man." Agnes was shaking her head, a sad expression on her face. "Fragile ego and all."

"I hate that it had to end like this," Garret continued, his voice taking on a tone of mock sorrow. "I'll be sure to tell them how I had to defend myself. That you came after me. And then I'll be gone. No one will be any the wiser."

"I do believe he is threatening you," Agnes said, her hands on her hips. "Poor form, sir."

"If only someone would help me," I said. Garret Goul's eyes narrowed, curious about my seemingly odd reply.

"Yeah," Agnes mused. "Now would be a great time for the hot detective to come bursting in."

I shot her a look that I hoped was conspicuous enough that Garret Goul wouldn't notice it.

"Oh, right! I'm on it. Mission, go get the hottie." Agnes vanished. Leaving me alone with a killer.

A killer who was quickly becoming impatient. "Give me my ring and I will be on my way."

Slowly, trying to drag out every moment, I removed the ring from my pocket. "How does this thing work?" I asked, speaking slower than a sloth would. "I mean I know about Darwin but what does he do?"

Garret's eyes narrowed in on the ring held in my hand. "The demon magic casts an illusion over those who it enchants. It makes them susceptible to suggestion. From there it's really simple to suggest that my patients don't do the thing that causes them to be oddities. It's also easy to make them express how incredible I am. I was, I mean. It was easy enough until that Banshee came along."

"Because Sabrina's power was within her," I stated. "It wasn't some external issue. I could simply not ever do magic again by your logic and then I would never know that my magic still didn't work. But Sabrina couldn't be fooled for long into thinking she couldn't hear the voices."

"Exactly," he tsked, softly under his breath. "You know, you missed your calling. You could do so much more than be your mother's little secretary. You're quite sharp."

"Thank you."

"Pity." Garret Goul reached forward and drew out a knife from beneath his pillow. The thing had to be about a foot long with a lethal-looking razor-sharp edge to it.

"Won't someone wonder how you were able to get a giant knife to defend yourself?" I took a step backward and bumped into the wall.

He shrugged. "People tend to not ask questions when they are in shock. I could always make them forget what they saw, too. That would be easy enough once my ring is back. Though I had good powers of persuasion already." He shook his head again, "It is a shame, of all the clients here this time, I liked you the best."

"Lucky me," I muttered.

Garret Goul sighed. "Goodbye, Poppy." He lunged toward me.

I let out a wild shriek and ducked to the side. The knife sliced into the wall where my ear had been moments before. I ducked and raced under his arm.

With the grace of a jungle cat, Garret Goul performed a wild leap over the bed. Managing to block my exit. He may as well have shouted "Parkour!" as he did it.

If it had been any other time, I would have been impressed. I could only dream of vaulting like that.

My breath caught in my throat as he raised the knife again.

I swallowed and called upon all the magic inside of me. Chaos and ordinary, weak and strong. Old magic and new magic. Every ounce of it I forced to the surface until I could feel it practically humming in my veins. Then I began to chant.

I held my hands up. "Peel of thunder, hear my plea, surround my soul, and protect me!"

There was a loud crack, followed by a howl, and then the crunch of something very large smashing into a tiny space.

I heard running feet and then the slamming of doors. It sounded like the cavalry was arriving. Silas skidded into the room and almost ended up tripping over the massive Galapagos tortoise, with giant fuzzy eyebrows, indicative of Garret Goul.

"What the hell?" Silas barked. He took a large step back as the tortoise snapped its jaws at him in fury. "Is that a turtle?"

"Tell the oaf that technically it's a tortoise. Turtles live in the sea and tortoises live on land. There's a difference," Agnes barked. "And tell him that he's not getting into your panties now."

"It's Garret Goul," I sighed. "I was trying a spell to protect myself from him, then poof, he's a tortoise." Uncontrolled Chaos.

"Garret Goul?" Silas asked. "But he's dead."

"Oh, do try to keep up," Agnes said, rolling her eyes. "I swear, everyone here is at least ten steps behind you, and you're not a detective."

"He's not dead. He was possessed, by this ring." I held it out, and the tortoise snapped its jaws at the sight of the ring. Silas quickly grabbed it. "Lyra and I found runes of protection under Garret Goul's bed and there are freshly carved ones under Darcy's bed here. That's because Garret Goul killed him, assumed his identity, and then killed Sabrina, who was the only one of us who would recognize him."

"But why?" Delilah had arrived, and behind her I could see Lyra and Sean all standing in the doorway.

"Because Garret Goul's power came from the ring and its enchantments. He couldn't fix problems. He could only mask them. The demon, Darwin, inside that ring could make people believe that they were cured. But in reality, they weren't. Darcy figured it out when Sabrina showed up, needing help again."

Silas turned the ring over in his fingers, his eyes looking anywhere but at me. I glanced down at the angry tortoise. "It wasn't my plan to turn him into a tortoise, but…" I shrugged. "I suspect he'll turn back sooner or later. Though since tortoises live longer than cats, it may be a while."

The clock on the wall of Darcy's bedroom chimed loudly in the gaping silence that followed. Twelve chimes for noon.

"That's right," Agnes sneered. "Stay quiet, you cowards. None of you were willing to help us find the truth and now we are going to walk out of here and you can deal with the giant tortoise in the room."

I shrugged my shoulders. "I assume I'm free to go," I asked Silas.

He nodded dumbly, and I walked past him. Agnes, I noticed, made sure to pass through him on her way out the door. Silas shuddered and I felt a little bit of glee. I walked down the hallway and to the heavy wooden front doors that were now standing ajar.

"Your exit would have been far less dramatic if the doors had still been locked," Agnes muttered.

24

What's a Girl to Do?

IT TOOK ME A week to get over everything that happened.

A whole week to feel better about the murders, being a suspect, feeling betrayed by a hot man, being put into handcuffs, solving the mystery by myself, nearly dying in the process, and proving my innocence.

I ignored all my mother's phone calls. I didn't want to talk to her about the experience. I knew that she'd probably heard the news through the grapevine, but she hadn't come and checked on me. It didn't bother me. I figured she wouldn't.

Agnes was pouting. Mostly about Silas. I think she was more disappointed in him than I was. It was a bit much, in my opinion. But it meant that she wasn't knocking things off the shelves like a deranged cat.

I got absorbed in reading a few books and crocheting mini-animals for Lyra. Surprisingly the Fae had become a good friend—even if she did have an obsession with small crafted things.

She called every day to check in, so at least I had someone who made me laugh and was as off-kilter as I was. Maybe I could convince her to move to a remote cabin with me and be off-griders. Or at least end up in the same nursing home together after we lived out our spinster lives. That would be fun.

I didn't hear anything from the Dartmoths. My guess is they went back to their mansion and were eating their vegetables as usual. I just hoped they were getting sideways glances from all their vampire family members.

I had just finished crocheting a trunk on a purple elephant when my doorbell rang.

I ignored it. It was probably more yarn or something. I had ordered a bunch from Amazon when I got home. Anything to distract myself.

The doorbell rang again.

"Ding-dong," Agnes shouted from the bedroom. "Ding-dong, ding-dong!"

I stood up from the couch, throwing the blanket off. "You'd be a better doorbell if you told me who it was."

"You could always get a video doorbell. That would be easier," she shouted back at me.

I sighed as I shuffled down the hallway.

"You can just leave the package on the porch," I said as I opened the door. "It's a good neighborhood. It wouldn't have gotten..." I trailed off because it wasn't the Amazon delivery guy. It also wasn't my mother, thank god.

Instead, Silas stood on the porch, coffee in one hand, and a bag that smelled suspiciously like donuts in the other.

I slammed the door.

It was a natural reaction. I was dressed in sweatpants and a tank top. My hair was in a messy bun, and I was wearing crocheted bunny slippers. They were pink and comfy and I loved that I had made them—even if the bunny's eyes were lopsided.

And Silas? Well, he was dressed in his uniform. He had just come from work, or was on his way to work. The man didn't have a hair out of place. Yes, his hair was short, so it was difficult to have a hair out of place, but still. He looked perfect and put together. And I was in bunny slippers.

"Is that the traitor?" Agnes asked, coming down the hall. "Does he look miserable and repentant?"

"He's got donuts."

Agnes gave me a critical look. "What is wrong with you?"

"He handcuffed me!"

"I didn't ask why you were upset. I know that and I agree. I asked what is wrong with you? You should have at least grabbed the donuts before closing the door."

"Agnes!" Silas called through the door. "I know you're there with her. Can you please open the door and let me in?"

Agnes snorted. "Tell him that just because he's a pretty boy doesn't mean that I forgive him. He thought you had killed someone, and by extension, he thought I was covering it up! That is so incredibly offensive to me and my kin."

"She says no," I shouted through the door.

"Tell him he needs to kiss my fanny. And perform a séance so I can see if he has any hot, dead ancestors."

"I'm not telling him that."

"Look," Silas shouted through the door. "I'm sorry. I'm sorry that I thought that you'd killed

Garret and Sabrina. But I knew if it had been you, it would have been an accident. But I had to be sure!"

"You didn't have to handcuff me! You could have just asked me straight out. Instead, you pretended to be interested in me. I told you about Agnes and you used it against me. Even if you did let me solve it, you should have stood up for me."

"You're right," Silas admitted. "I was hoping at every turn of events that it wasn't you. I was trying to reason with myself and tell myself that it wasn't you, but there was evidence. I was trying to make sure that you were safe. I'm sorry that I handcuffed you. I promise I won't do it again, without your permission."

There was a pause on the other side of the door. "I think you're amazing, Poppy. I was so impressed with how you solved the whole thing yourself. And without help from me, the one who was supposed to solve it. I love how, at every turn, you tried to see the good in people, even when they were accusing you of malice. I love how you protect Agnes's presence so that others can't make fun of her. I'm here because I want to be with you. Take you out on a date. But I also understand that you might need time. I will keep trying. But for now, I'll leave the donuts and tea on your porch. When you're ready to talk, I'll be waiting."

I heard the brush of a bag being set down on the steps and then muted footsteps as he began walking away.

I looked over at Agnes, who looked conflicted. "What do you think?"

Agnes bit her lip and frown lines appeared on her forehead. "I don't like what he did."

"I don't either."

"But he did come here and apologize. And it was a pretty impressive speech."

"It was."

"Maybe we could listen to him. Maybe let him feed us dinner." Agnes was waffling back and forth. "It doesn't have to mean that we fully forgive him. But, as long as no one dies around us, and he doesn't try to handcuff us again, then maybe we can consider going out with him."

I sighed and opened the door.

Silas was halfway back to his police SUV. At the sound of the door opening, he turned and looked at me.

He had a hopeful expression on his face, and when he saw my bunny slippers, a smile slid across his face. "Nice slippers."

"Are you free tonight?" I asked. "Agnes says you can take me out, if you are."

The small smile became a full-blown grin. "I sure am free, and I would love to take you out. You like Mexican food?"

"Who doesn't?"

"Freaks."

"And the two of us certainly aren't freaks. The Chaos queen and the wonder pup."

"I like that name, wonder pup, I may make the pack call me that."

"Tell them I came up with it."

"Of course I will. Credit where credit is due. They're already giving me a hard time for not solving the case, and being shown up by a little brainiac witch. This will just add to it."

"Someone should be giving you a hard time. You got it super wrong."

"Incredibly wrong." Silas grinned. "I will always admit that. But it looks like something good is going to be coming out of that. Shall I pick you up at five?"

"Yes."

"Good. Wear the slippers."

"I will not be wearing the slippers."

"But they're cute."

"Shut up and say 'thank you' to Agnes. She also wants to know if you have a hot dead ghost somewhere in your family tree."

"Thank you, Agnes, for convincing our girl to give me a chance. And I'll look for one. Don't know how I'd get him here, but I can try."

"That's all I ask for," I said. "I'll see you at five."

"See you then, Chaos Queen."

***

The End

Acknowledgments

So many people have encouraged me to write this book.

My husband, who gave me time to write—even when we had a newborn at home. I love you and am so thankful for your encouragement and patience. Thanks for listening to me talk about things and bounce ideas off you, and for looking up random things (like blond and blonde).

My mom, who is also my editor. Thank you for all the time and painstaking effort you have put into this (and raising me, but that deserves an entirely different letter). You have taught me to be a go-getter and to try my best. Thanks for encouraging my dreams and doing everything in your power to make it happen. Any grammar mistakes in this book are my own.

My dad, for thinking everything I write is awesome, even when it isn't. Thanks for doing chores around the house while Mom and I talked about the book, and for just being a constant source of encouragement.

For my son, I love you so much. I want you to know that you should always try hard things, and that the things that scare you are also the most worthwhile. I hope one day when you see this, you'll think it's cool that your mom wrote a book.

To the numerous friends and family members who have heard me talk about this project, thanks so much for listening. I'm so thankful for each and every one of you.

To the reader, I hope you enjoyed this book. If you could kindly leave a review, I would deeply appreciate it.

Much love,

Kathryn

About the Author

 Kathryn Roberson is a mother, wife, author, and teacher who lives with her family in beautiful Washington State. She has spent nine years teaching elementary school and has loved every minute of it. She enjoys encouraging students to write what they love. Kathryn is an avid reader and has a passion for teaching science.

Kathryn always dreamed of writing a book and used to tell herself stories to pass the time as a kid. It wasn't until she gave birth to her son, that she finally worked up the nerve to publish her first children's chapter book, *The Case of the Missing Ring: a June-Bug Doggie Detective Mystery.* She then published four more children's chapter books all following the adventures of her golden retriever, June-Bug. You can find the whole series on Amazon.

This is the first adult book that she has published. You can find her on her Instagram (though she isn't the best at updating it), and YouTube at K.S.Roberson.Author